BURNING DOWN THE HOUSE

BURNING DOWN THE HOUSE

MERRY MCINERNEY

A TOM DOHERTY ASSOCIATES BOOK
NEW YORK

BURNING DOWN THE HOUSE

Copyright © 1994 by Merry McInerney

This book is printed on acid-free paper.

A Forge Book
Published by Tom Doherty Associates, Inc.
175 Fifth Avenue
New York, N.Y. 10010

Design by Lynn Newmark

Library of Congress Cataloging-in-Publication Data

McInerney, Merry.
    Burning down the house / Merry McInerney.
        p.   cm.
    "A Tom Doherty Associates book."
    ISBN 0-312-85698-9
    1. Authors' spouses—New York (N.Y.)—Fiction.
    2. Married women—New York (N.Y.)—Fiction.
    3. Manhattan (New York, N.Y.)—Fiction.   I. Title.
PS3563.C36945B87   1994
813'.54—dc20   94-12925
                                                         CIP

First edition: September 1994

Printed in the United States of America

0   9   8   7   6   5   4   3   2   1

A NOTE TO THE READER:

This is a work of fiction. In this book, though some characters and events are inspired by people and events in my life, I do not intend them to be actual representations of these people or events, and they certainly should not be taken as such.

For example, though the character I call "Blase Regenhere" shares with my ex-husband the broad characteristic of publishing a successful first novel, in most every other respect they differ.

In sum, this is a work of fiction and should not be considered to contain factual representations of people or events in my life.

For my mother

*I wish to express my deepest gratitude
to Elena Delbanco, Andrew Morse,
Charles Kaiser, Ron Messerich,
Susan Contratto, Terry Holmes,
Lori Perkins, Emile Borde, Robin Harnist,
the Doctors LeBel, Courtney Yoder, and
Robert and Barbara Reymond for their
kindness, wisdom, and encouragement
during the writing of this book.*

Contents

BURNING DOWN THE HOUSE

ONE

The End

Here's how he put it to me: "I'm leaving. I'm not in love with you. There's nothing to continue this marriage for. I love Agnes. Good-bye."

I was stymied—no, I was bamboozled. Maybe flummoxed. The brain lurched, reeled, and lay stunned and gaping in my head until those infelicitous words poked it again and it flipflopped, whacking against the inside of my skull like an echo.

You can imagine my shock, my outrage, my indignation when I tell you the guy was a *writer*—not just any writer, but *Blase Regenhere*, author of the smartest, hippest, shortest novel to reach number four on *The Gotham Daily*'s Best Seller List in 1983. (Although sometimes I call him "Blasé" and other people mistakenly call him "Blahs," you say his first name "Blaze." The surname should be pronounced, "Rayner," though most people say "Regen-here" and everyone misspells it. Blase insists it's Old English, but it looks pretty German to me.)

In case you haven't read it (though they say Everyone has), Blase's claim to literary fame is *A Dark*

Night of the Soul: a slim sordid tale about the jaunty escapades of a thirty-eight-year-old New York fop who flushes his brain in toiletfuls of whiskey, is fired from his modest job as assistant instructor at Fordham University but conceals it from his wife and friends, fearing they'll tell him he's a self-indulgent, asshole alcoholic, and lures his dates to a seedy motel on the wrong side of some bridge where they do it doggy-style. Of course, the boy/man (this is a Coming of Age story, also) has to make a career change and becomes a purveyor of illicit substances, though he tells his wife, who's sweet, dowdy, and unsuspecting (because stupid—all the women in the book are basically stupid bimbos cooing things like "Gee, you're a saint!") that he's a headhunter now, must receive a wide array of clients, at home, in privacy, at almost any time of the day or night. And *that*? That's a pharmaceutical scale he uses for illustrative purposes. Not much happens in the middle: we see the boy/man sell cocaine, we see the boy/man drink whiskey, we see the boy/man sniff cocaine, we see the boy/man lie, we see the boy/man steal, we see the boy/man sniff more cocaine, we notice the boy/man has become a cocaine addict; then the boy/man suddenly remembers his childhood pup, Comet, who ran away one rainy morning, which helps bring him to the brink of a critical piece of self-knowledge which, naturally, is saved for the denouement. The ending is meant to be redemptive and cathartic: the boy/man, now financially as well as morally bankrupt, friendless, fat and wrinkled and wearing synthetic fibers, awakens one morning on the fire escape of a one-room apartment occupied by three

Hispanic families and a blond Hindu woman, whom he assumes he slept with. The Hindu woman turns out to be a Trinidadian who confesses to having crabs and tries to con money off him for Kwell; the boy/man finally agrees to trade her his Gold Card for a cup of coffee, which turns out to be not only instant but decaf, and the boy/man thinks how the whole world is deception. And then, in the greasy, grey light of early morning, the boy/man comes to the profound, heartbreaking realization that he *is*, after all, nothing more than a self-indulgent, asshole alcoholic and drug addict and he pukes.

"A Must-to-Read! . . . *the* novel of the eighties."

"Rib-tickling and hair-raising, like a ride on a runaway train."

"Heart-wrenching . . . a desperate cry for meaning in a world that's run amok."

These were some of the things people said about the book. They dubbed Blase "Yuppie Oracle of the Nouvelle Vague," "C.O. of the Celebrated New Inksquirters," and "Mouthpiece of the Me-First Generation." He was reputed to be "handsome" and "dapper," and though no one went so far as to call him "adonic," a reporter from Rhode Island insisted he was "princely." I certainly wouldn't deny Blase had his charms—I'd married him, after all—but, honestly, they weren't to be found in his appearance. Objectively, he was at best and at worst pretty goofy-looking: though his waist was long and narrow, so were his head and chest; he had the bulky thighs of a soccer player, which quickly tapered into calves as thin

17

as birthday candles stuck in two very wide, very thick, very stumpy feet that put me in mind of lower-case *d*'s. Unless packed with gels or slicked with pomade, his thick blond hair stood high on his head, like pale cotton candy. Undoubtedly, his finest feature was his eyes: they were a light grey, as round and luminous as two sulphide marbles, as guileless as gum balls, a nose length apart, and, with his blond lashes and brows, he always had a startled look which was very engaging. But handsome Blase was not, though, as I say, he had his charms.

Everyone wanted to interview Blase; Everyone wanted to take him to lunch and watch him get loaded; Everyone wanted to photograph him with his arms around hookers in front of sleazy strip joints or reclining seductively in designer jeans on bricks of pressed baby powder. People recognized him on the street; they mispronounced his name at cocktail parties and chichi fund-raisers. *The Gotham Daily* gave him his own column, "In and Out." He was hired to do magazine endorsements for products like sunglasses, cognac, and a nasal decongestant. And, naturally, Hollywood called: Everyone out there loved him, too. But these events come later, toward the end of the story.

Here I was, then, after four years of for-better-for-worse, being given the heave-ho by *the* wordsmith of his generation, and the best he can give me at this signal, pivotal moment is: "I'm leaving. I'm not in love with you. There's nothing to continue this marriage for. I love Agnes. Good-bye." Though his characters (the males, I mean) were breathtakingly quick with the *bon mot*, the off-the-cuff witticism, the snappy come back, Blase himself was not. Still, he'd had plenty of time to prepare himself and one might have thought he'd have taken the trouble to steal something from Shakespeare or Yeats, something sweet and sad but consoling, something like

> Sweetest love, I do not go,
> For weariness of thee,
> Nor in hope the world can show
> A fitter love for me.

Then again, Blase was never very good at endings.

After he slammed the front door, left me on my knees in the foyer (a pathetic, desperate measure, I know, and it never worked in the movies either), I went through it again, just in case he'd dropped some subtle clue about loving *me* and leaving *Agnes*. Taking the first word from each sentence, I got: "I'm I'm there's I good-bye." Meaningless, I decided, except maybe to a Hegelian, which Blase wasn't.

I did better with the final words: "Leaving you for Agnes Good-bye" but decided that couldn't have been the secret message since that's what he'd already said. Next I went for anagrams, but stopped when I got: "I want to have the note. I'm going to sue you." I was projecting—it was *me* who wanted the note; it was *me* who was going to sue.

After Blase slammed the door behind him, like a full stop, like a QED at the end of a proof, left me wretched and trembling like a terrier genuflected in the entranceway, I finally got to my feet and scrambled down the hall to his study and began screaming at his image on the wall, screaming what seemed, even then, to be the hackneyed recriminations of a soap opera star: "You *left* me?" "How could you leave me?" "Don't leave me!" "God, *please* come back." Awful things like that.

I took the seat at his desk and began to examine all his little things: the photograph of Blase as a baby, drooly and sanguine and toothless in bonnet and sunsuit, playing on the beach with his dog Bruno; his Boston/KS pencil sharpener leaking shavings from the "Standard" hole; a paper clip, twisted into an *S*, wrapped with a green elastic band, spearing a wad of yellow paper; his tiny Japanese plate with the lanky frog embracing a blade of grass; and his windup toys—there must have been a dozen of them: a gorilla that did flips, a boxing kangaroo, a choo-choo train, a clanging alarm clock, a dinosaur that spit sparks, a walking pair of lips, a telephone that rang, chattering teeth, a tiny space shuttle that disgorged astronauts, a winking eye, a book that opened and shut, and a little sports car that made a sound like breaking glass when it zoomed into something. To focus his attention while he wrote, Blase would crank up all the toys, set everything in motion, and wherever I was in the apartment I'd hear the tinkle, clank, jingle, buzz, whir, and whiz of my husband hard at work. I've found it's things like that, things that used to make you grit your teeth and flay your palms, the annoying habits and irritating quirks (his constant rocking while he spoke, the snap of his fingers when he concluded a story), that take on a larger reference in retrospect, become endearing and almost mythic for having marked and sustained the pulse and rhythm of daily life, like a metronome, like a beating heart.

I wound up all the toys and really worked myself into a lather, sobbing in that ugly, graceless, heaving way I have which Blase says makes me look like Lon Chaney and sound like a victim of black lung. And just as a calm would begin to settle over me and my gasping and retching would ease into panting and hiccuping, I would look up and see baby Blase playing on the sand with his doggy, and shriek and begin the gasping and retching thing anew. It wasn't nostalgia or a broken heart that powered me back into hysteria—those feelings come later, when you really, finally believe It's Over and then you get a chance to go into paroxysms all over again, for months even. Rather, a question as innocent as a frying pan smacked me full in the face: *What do I do now?* For an hour I continued with the hysterics, and when my seizures would subside into a pant-hiccup-pant-hiccup, I'd just glance at that photo and renew my efforts.

The photo had a special power to pain me, since two years ago, quite unexpectedly, I got this intense yearning to vomit in the morning and waddle around with hand affixed to the small of my back, to dribble thimblefuls of pee on my panties when I laughed or sneezed—in short, to reproduce, which desire seemed impossible; surely I'd been duped by some base and primal hormones. But it also struck me as utterly enchanting and singularly alluring.

Shortly after we were married, I began to have a recurrent, erotic dream about motherhood: I am sit-

21

ting, naked, nursing or simply cradling my baby in a rosy light. That's it; the whole dream. It came in two styles—conservative (my hair up, my baby wrapped in a blanket, me sitting in a rocking chair) and liberal (my hair down, my baby nude, me sitting on the floor)—and I would wake from it warm and wet and full of passion.

At first, Blase thought it was a great idea—progeny! Someone to remember him and correctly pronounce his name! A symbol of fertility, prosperity, and the Good Life. But after a few months, he seemed to have a change of heart. Sometimes I told myself this was why our marriage soured.

Blase must have seen his departure as an imperative epistemic escape, my presence having become for him a hideous but undeniable assertion. After all, I'd read the note from James Hartley and Blase knew I'd read the note and I knew he knew I'd read the note and I knew he was lying about James and lying about the note and he knew I knew he was lying about James and lying about the note and, fact is, Blase was just never very comfortable with too much knowledge. Undoubtedly he justified his abrupt exit by telling himself he was performing a truly authentic act, he was exercising his limitless Sartrean free will, he was *de bonne foi*. Surely he added to this justification something about it being for my own good. Now he was free. He would move in with Agnes, Asian-American Actress, vapid, aging, erstwhile star of Spam commercials and scantily clad screamer in tawdry horror flicks, who was clingy and servile since Martin

McSwane, B-film czar and producer of such classics as *Demon Babies in Daycare*, roped some prime tenderloin and put old Agnes out to pasture. Giggly and fatuous, Agnes penned insipid, childish messages on heart-shaped note paper and in the books she gave Blase. The fool would save every note in his sock drawer, which, naturally, I would find and, naturally, I would swipe. They voiced the silly sentiments of a chick who was gaga about her guy, in the highfalutin, overwrought language of a gum-snapping teenager, expressive of the sort of cast of mind that prompts men to call women "girls." They contained nonsense like "4-ever" and "I ♥ U" and one was even a "roses are red" poem. I got enormous satisfaction the afternoon I discovered an apparently flawless first edition of *A Portrait of the Artist*, flipped to the title page, and saw, in her curlicue handwriting:

Honey-bun,

My love is like a star. It's bright and twinkly and it will burn on and on. This is a really great book—and so are you.

Kiss-hug,
Agnes

After about an hour of sitting at Blase's desk, trying to keep my attention on Blase, on the fact that he'd just left me, *abandoned* me, thoughts, mostly trivial and unrelated, oddly juxtaposed, like what you see from a spinning ride at the amusement park, began a steeplechase in my head: *Toilet's running . . . haven't*

checked the mail . . . he left me; I've been left . . . lunch
with David at two . . . toilet's running . . . how could
he leave me . . . call plumber . . . Two. Lunch. David
*. . . son of a bitch . . . pimple on my chin . . . *until I
thought of Agnes.

I'd seen her once, one afternoon when I'd come
home early from school. She was sneaking out of our
apartment with her shoes in one hand (as if I were
asleep in the hall—idiot), a shopping bag from Saks in
the other. She didn't say anything. I didn't say anything, but I checked her out. There was a tangle of
carpet fluff and hair and God-knows-what-else on the
sleeve of her coat—slob—and she was wearing cheap,
gaudy earrings of colored glass and fake pearls. And
she was flat. Everything about her was flat. Her face
was round and flat. Her tiny nose was flat. Her head
was flat. Her very chest was flat, flat, flat. (I wondered
if Blase consoled her with "more than a handful is a
waste" in the same sincere voice he'd once used to
assure me that "there's more to love"—jerk.)

One unhappy quality I've observed in myself and others is that when unexpectedly cast in certain roles,
roles of people isolated and vulnerable—like being the
driver of a car in midtown at rush hour, or being the
cuckolded spouse—an alarming degree of self-
restraint is required to avoid acting like an out-and-
out asshole. Though you may really be the kind of
person who cares for her fellow man, who generally
says, "After you" and yields, who usually stops to
assist a person in distress, in this new role you may
suddenly find yourself honking your horn, waving

your arms, pounding the dash, screaming invectives, railing in vain like Lear against the storm, against what is not in your control, until movement in time and space brings you to a new place and you return to your self.

Though when I found out about Agnes I cried and stomped my feet and threw a banana at Blase, called her horrible names and threatened illegal acts of harassment, I knew, even then, that the object of my fury was not Agnes. I did not care that *she* occupied the role of the Other Woman but that *someone* occupied that role, that Blase had allowed someone to occupy that role, and that someone's occupying that role meant that I now occupied this role and that terms like "estranged" and "abandoned" might now be applied to me. But, truth is, I had already gotten used to this idea because I had learned about Agnes's presence in Blase's life after I had discovered the note. *The note.*

I started with his desk. His drawers were a mess of papers, postcards, thumbtacks, gum balls, rubber bands, a stiff piece of French bread, expired credit cards, two Quaaludes, a bar of rabbit-shaped soap, writing instruments, used Kleenex, envelopes folded from pages of magazines still dusted with a sparkly white, unanswered correspondence, and, for some reason, a can of tomato paste. I emptied them onto the floor, combed through all the junk. Then his bookcases—paper scraps and old photographs (I found two of Agnes, on which I drew mustaches and devil horns) and cash register receipts were stuck between the pages or slipped under the jackets, but no note. On the bottom shelf I found his journals with frayed and rounded corners, covers mottled like malted Easter eggs. I began to read: *"Last week I met a remarkable woman, an impressionist painter, intelligent, witty, sexy, and absolutely stunning. Oh, to live in a world where I could fuck Arlene Miller! But, of course, there's Agnes to consider."* Agnes? I reread the passage. The entry was dated two months ago. Had I been nobody for so long? With my teeth I tore the page from the notebook, chucked the notebook against the wall. In his other journals I found invitations to swanky parties, a sheet of toilet paper with *"Tangier"* written on it, cardboard coasters from bars in Hawaii and Key West, business cards with telephone numbers and cryptic messages *("What a slavedriver!")* scribbled on them, and two receipts for express mail to James Hartley with James's phone number entered in the "phone number" space. I could call him. Oh, yes, I could.

Blase's bureau drawers were practically empty except for a handful of foreign coins and mateless socks and underwear whose elastic had given out—obviously Blase had been sneaking shit to Agnes's—but in a shoe box forgotten under the bed I found a sterling silver pen, a brand new ostrich wallet, a pair of boxer shorts sprinkled with hearts, his Phi Beta Kappa key, and a pair of gold cuff links, all of which I promptly locked in my jewelry case—except for the shorts, of course, which I tossed down the incinerator. In his closet he'd left only his Brooks Brothers shirts and two blazers, from the old days, a tie, a pair of world-weary tassel loafers, and the crocodile shoes he'd had made for his stub-feet in Milan. I grabbed the crocs, ran out to the incinerator chute, and dropped them in too.

We had a storage space in the basement of the building, and there I discovered five cardboard boxes sealed with packing tape and addressed to Blase in care of Agnes. He'd packed several of our wedding gifts, including the antique silver service for twelve, some bath linens, the photos I'd taken of him with famous new friends, silk flowers, his erotic Japanese prints (thank God), my complete works of Dickens and Twain, and all the books we would have fought over: the rare, first, and limited editions, some inscribed to both of us. I lugged all the boxes upstairs, resealed them, and addressed them to my old college friend Rosie Ripberger in Seattle. No note.

For the next few days, or weeks, maybe, I wandered through the apartment disconnected and dazed, like I feel when I've just come back from a trip, or recovered from an illness. Everything I saw, everything I thought, I seemed to be seeing and thinking for the first time: Here, this is a scrapbook, a wedding band quilt, an extra set of keys. This is what it feels like to be drunk. This is what it feels like when no one's coming home. Like a thief, or a child left alone for the first time, I peeked in cabinets and closets, opened drawers, examined the paintings and photographs on the walls, the chachkas in the living room, the views from various windows. I tried on the old clothes in Blase's closet, walked around in his loafers, pulled his square man's brush through my hair. I turned the kitchen appliances on and off, thumbed through the records

27

and CDs and video cassettes. When the phone rang, I let the answering machine get it and eavesdropped: David wanted to know why I'd stood him up—was everything okay?; a special order for Blase had arrived at some store with an Italian name; my best friend Claire just had to tell me about the Hell's Angel she'd met last week who single-handedly jump-started her sex life; my mother wanted to say hi and to tell Blase and me she loved us, was thinking of us, and were we still coming up for her birthday? I spent a lot of time sitting in the front hall, staring at the door, sipping wine, hearing the relentless slamming of doors all through the apartment building, and Blase's voice: "Don't laugh; I'm *serious*. Will you marry me?" And I never once thought of the Blase who had betrayed me, to whom that note had been addressed, the Blase who had left me for the safety of Agnes's duplex—he was no one to me yet. I remembered the Blase of the old days.

Two

First Impressions

A man wearing a gold ring in his nose and a Mötley Crüe T-shirt threw up on his date.

"Lively party, huh?" I turned to see the blond boy beside me, unfashionably preppy in a navy crewneck sweater and jeans, which I liked. Propped at the edge of the couch, the boy was leaning forward, at an angle, toward me, resting his elbows on his thighs, hands folded in the space between his knees, as if he were explaining something to a very small child or perched on the toilet. The boy sniffled, plugged a nostril with the knuckle of his thumb, and sniffled again.

"Got a cold?" I said.

"Yeah, every weekend." Laughing loudly and oddly, like hayek-yek-yek, the boy bounced a few inches off the cushion as if he were getting to his feet, then fell against the back of the couch, rocked a couple of times, and snapped his fingers. He smiled and sniffled again and swallowed hard and all this time he was chewing his teeth and sliding his jaw side-to-side.

Oh, cocaine, I thought naively, which made me feel self-righteous, which made me feel like a square.

The boy, who I realized was a man because of his crow's feet and the ring of flab around his middle, said his name was Blase Regenhere—maybe I'd heard of him? Maybe not. He explained that he was an English professor at Columbia, his third Ivy League teaching gig in ten years, he said, had published several fairly influential articles in the *Voice*. He told a lot of outrageous stories, too outlandish to possibly be true, a schoolboy's tales of uproarious adventure and shocking exploits, referring to women as "girls" and twice alluding to bust size, tossing in a lot of names of apparently famous friends—his good buddy This and his crazy pal That—people I'd never heard of. He spoke very loudly, evidently addressing the room, waving his arms, lurching back and forth and snapping his fingers for emphasis. Some people stared. Some laughed. Others scowled and made a *snick* sound with their tongues. I thought he was an ass.

"Want another?" Blase said, gesturing at my beer bottle.

"Okay."

We were at the apartment of David Eastman, my childhood buddy, the first boy I'd kissed, the first person I got drunk with, someone who had known me when I was moon-faced and wrapped in baby fat. Unlike Blase, David was definitely what you'd call a looker; though no individual feature would, on its own, draw a crowd, all together, his deep brown eyes, his shiny brown hair, his slim body, and the graceful way he moved it had a thrilling effect. David was kind and lovable, had a genuine gift for story telling, a tender, mellifluous voice, and a wild passion for country music. He'd just moved to the city to get his MFA at Columbia, which was where he'd met Blase.

After Blase had been gone fifteen minutes, I noticed a smell apparently emanating from my left. Then, in the lurid red party light, I spotted the mountain of empty beer bottles heaped in the corner like a pile of dirty laundry. Beer bottles were lined up like targets on David's stereo and TV, on the otherwise barren shelves of his bookcase; grease-stained pizza boxes were poised precariously on a speaker; Styrofoam take-out containers were stacked on the side table like conversation pieces. And by the far wall, four unhappy paper bags sat in a row in a yellow tub, like my sisters and me when we were little, as if waiting for the mom to come and bathe them.

Funny David had become such a slob. He'd always been fastidious to the point of being obsessive-compulsive. We'd be playing chess in his room, nearing the end of a two-day cutthroat game or preparing to sneak out into the woods with a blanket and tingly lips, when he'd suddenly say, "Excuse me," and begin to dust or vacuum, alphabetize his high school notebooks, or simply move an object from here to there. David was the only person I had known who pressed his underwear, aside from my sister Kate, the Neat One. (I was the Smart One, by default, since Anne was undeniably the Pretty One, Isabelle had dubbed herself the Artistic One before I got a chance at it, while I was still the Little One, and my parents were running out of laudatory adjectives—and, no, Isabelle, they were simply *not* going to call me the Fat One.) Funny how things change.

Hank Williams was singing "Settin' the Woods on Fire" but people were stiff-armed and spastic, bouncing up and down, jerking their bodies like ECT patients, as if powered by the rhythms of a punk band with one of those violent names like StabUinDaFace or DrawnNKwarturd. Doing the monkey by the bathtub was Della Kramer, New Age retro-hippie and the only other philosophy grad student present, who wore her bacon-colored hair shaved on one side of her head, woven in a long thin braid on the other. She sported Birkenstock sandals, peace signs on her ears, and designer jeans, and spent all her time on Heidegger and Fichte and insisted on sharing her conclusions with me: "Oh! The being of the being-for, once viewed as of-the-world, is the formal mode of the Being!"

Della hurried over and introduced her boyfriend, a greying man in his fifties wearing trapezoidal sideburns, a three-piece suit, and a "Save the Lemur" pin, as "Harry, my significant other." They were just leaving, Della regretted to say; maybe I'd like to join them for carrot sandwiches at New Dawn?

"It's atmospherically intense," Della said. "They have ionized air and only play Kitaro tapes, man."

I thanked her anyway.

About thirty people who all knew each other and had agreed to ignore me had formed a big circle around David, who was singing loudly, sweetly, and everyone was dancing or chatting and laughing.

I picked up a stereo magazine from the end table and began looking through it as if that were my purpose in being there, I'd *come* to see this catalogue, I'd *die* if I didn't get the latest on graphic equalizers.

What happened to my beer?

Someone tapped me on the shoulder. A pale, sweaty man wearing a T-shirt with a cocaine vial silk-screened on the front and underneath it, "A Line Is a Terrible Thing to Waste," had seated himself next to me on the couch. He was grinning. He winked. "Hey!" he said.

I gave him the quick smile I give people to put them off, to let them know I'm very busy with something, which my sister Isabelle, with her delicate sensibility, says makes me look like I'm trying to fart, which, now that I think about it, might be the reason it actually does put people off. But maybe because of the noxious odors already pervading the air, the man was not deterred.

He asked my name. "Toby Dodge." He asked what I did. "I'm getting my doctorate in philosophy at NYU." I always forgot to lie at moments like this, but then I hadn't apprenticed under Blase yet so hadn't quite mastered the art, though I'd never be really good at it, like him. For Blase, however, lying wasn't a mere habit, a finite series of recurrent behaviors like a repeating pattern on a bolt of cloth; it was a matter of reflex, involuntary and persistent as the hiccups. Of course, Blase would lie when he felt he should, to avoid hurting people's feelings. Blase also lied when he felt he had to, to weasel out of a sticky situation. To avoid moral or legal accountability, to impress or challenge or comfort or wound, Blase would lie. Blase lied for the sake of a good story, a good laugh, or a good lay. And when absolutely nothing was at stake, when you'd simply asked where something was or had he ever read *Lorna Doone*, you could catch Blase lying. In fact, Blase's lying was so pervasive that were you to preface anything that came out of his mouth with "It's not the case that," you would have a perfectly reliable truth-tracking machine. Not that I could have known any of this yet.

"Philosophy?" the man said. "Here's my philosophy: fuck 'em if they can't take a toke." He laughed, put his hand on my knee, and said, "No, seriously. My philosophy is you always gotta look out for yourself first."

"An ethical egoist."

"Not an *egoist*. Just a realist."

I bristled. I took a breath and launched into my standard defense of absolutist ethical objectivism, part-swiped from Plato, part-swiped from the *Nicomachean Ethics*, the rest based on indefensible metaphysical and epistemological assumptions and unjustified optimism. I said, "Look . . . "; I said, "Listen . . . " I threw in principles of second-order and modal logics, offered up premises he couldn't say no to since they contained technical terms he wouldn't understand, and moreover, I wouldn't shut up, I couldn't shut up. Once I got going on these tirades they took on a life of their own, and like my innocent audience I'd be staring at myself, aghast, wondering where all this was leading, wondering what I'd say next, wondering what I was getting so heated up about.

"And that's the proof of my second claim—that saying something is good or bad for a person doesn't commit one to any form of ethical relativism. In fact, I'll show you that this is, on the contrary, *inconsistent* with relativism and actually entails the truth of ethical absolutism." This was me speaking.

I argued my position into the ground, enlisting as alleged allies Kant, Hobbes, Nietzsche, even Wittgenstein, philosophers who no more agreed with my position than I understood theirs. Then, feeling my territory well defended, I turned and swashbuckled across his, attacking so ruthlessly that the man finally snorted through his nose and retreated, leaving me exhausted and angry and resentful at having so pointlessly and dishonestly mauled a stranger, a layman, an innocent. Suddenly feeling even more alone on the couch, I began to recite a familiar refrain of self-pity: *I am twenty-seven, single, and childless. The backs of my thighs are beginning to look like they're padded with oatmeal. My contribution to humanity is tinkering with definitions and arguments, a self-serving pursuit even if I did out-Webster Webster. The name on my birth certificate is Hermione.*

Where was my beer?

Standing near the bathtub, leaning into his hip, was a tall man with long, wavy hair and Buddy Holly glasses, talking to a Chinese girl in a black dress hemmed with ball fringe, comparing himself to Plato, "Except, of course, for what he said about the poets. I'll just *never* be able to forgive him for *that*." I went for the bottle I'd left on the end table, resigning myself to the last warm, foamy sip, and saw a legion of ants, black and glossy, swarming up its side. I flipped the bottle onto the mountain in the corner and with it most of the ants, leaving a spoonful in a riot of indecision. That appalling, nauseating feeling overcame me again (*I am lonely. I will always be lonely. I will die alone.*) and I felt raw and cold and at the point of bolting when Blase suddenly materialized, smiling, a beer bottle raised in each hand like fresh catch.

"Voilà!" he said.

"You speak French?"

"Is Ed Koch gay?" he said, snapping his fingers.

"I don't know."

"Me neither." Blase laughed loudly again, snapped his fingers.

"So do you?"

"Do I what?" Blase said.

"Speak French."

"Mais oui," he said.

"Moi, j'en parle seulement un peu. Je l'ai etudié à l'école secondaire et aussi à l'université jusqu'au point que j'ai découvert la philosophie. Alors, maintenant, pour la plupart, je l'ai oublié de trop. Où l'as-tu etudié?" I asked.

"Of course, I'm a bit rusty now." Laugh. Snap. "So what do you do?"

"Study philosophy."

"*Really?* No kidding. Me, too. I mean, I dabble in philosophy, too. Hey, a piece of advice: stay with it. Call me old-fashioned, but I follow Plato on this. Man's essence is to exercise virtue in accordance with perfect reason."

"You probably mean 'to exercise reason in accordance with perfect virtue,' " I said, "but that's not quite right."

"Right," Blase said.

"And that was Aristotle."

"I meant Aristotle." Blase cleared his throat. "As I was saying—what was I saying?"

"You were saying 'Stick with it' and then you said—"

"Ah yes!" Blase slapped the top of his head. "Undoubtedly some cretin swine will try to talk you into majoring in something practical, like business or engineering, something that will get you a stuffed mattress and a well-lined wallet, but I say, hey! You're a girl. Why do you need to make money?"

"Girls have to eat, too, you know."

Blase slapped his forehead. "Christ! Next you'll be telling me they shit."

When he saw that I wasn't smiling, Blase squeezed my knee. "Sorry. I just meant that an attractive girl like you shouldn't have any trouble finding a man to support her."

"What would make you think that's what I'm looking for?"

Blase sniffled and stroked his nostrils with his forefinger. "Whatever," he said. "Just don't let anyone talk you out of getting the BA."

"I have my BA. I'm working on my doctorate."

"Hot damn!" Blase said. He bounced on the couch, nodding, and added something about how the French philosophers were the way to go.

"There are no French philosophers," I said.

"What about Camus and Sartre?"

"They weren't really philosophers."

"What about Descartes?" Blase added.

"He wasn't really French."

Blase lowered his eyebrows and seemed on the verge of begging to differ, then laughed. "So which philosophers do you like?" he said.

"Dead or alive?"

"Let's just say still warm."

"Well, Quine, of course. And Kripke. Putnam. Certainly Bennett. Oh, and Lewis—I really admire his work. Nagel, Kaplan, Messerich, Dennett . . . "

I noticed a certain look had frozen on Blase's face: his mouth was opened slightly, his pupils dilated, his eyebrows raised. When I'd finished my list, he blinked.

"Of course," he said. "The usual suspects." He filled his mouth with beer and swallowed. "So what's your thesis about?"

"Personal identity and essence."

"Can you be more specific?"

"Really?"

"Fire away."

"Well, using Plantinga's view of the logic of possible worlds, I'm trying to defend an Aristotelian account of persons as essentially human beings, not possibly disembodied or brains in vats."

"What!" Blase said. "I'm *not* a brain in a vat? Wait till my mom hears about this!"

I ignored him. "And I try to work out a theory of diachronic identity—in some ways surprisingly similar to Parfit's—and to draw out further implications concerning the ontological status of organisms as opposed to inanimate objects and artifacts."

"I see," Blase said, leaning back into the couch, kicking a foot, nodding. "But have you considered what Nietzsche would say about all this?"

"I can't see he'd have *anything* to say about this."

Blase rocked forward, laughing, as if I'd made a joke. Then he snapped his fingers. "Wanna dance?"

"No, thanks."

"Hey, man." The qualified Platonist with the long, wavy hair and Buddy Holly glasses was holding out his hand and Blase shook it.

"Jib Foster," Blase said, "this is—"

"Toby Dodge," I said to Jib's shoulder as he was now looking toward the door, checking out new arrivals.

"Great," Jib said, turning back to Blase. "Put on your snowshoes, sport—major squalls have been sighted. Here's the script: Lissa, John, and I split for Heartbreak, stopping at Ali's to enlist her help in weathering the storm. You've been cast as benefactor and mentor and the curtain's rising. Entonces, ¡vámonos!"

"Better send in my understudy," Blase said.

"Understand: I'm talking *blizzard*. Your kind of weather, sport."

"At the moment I believe I'm feeling the need for a more temperate clime."

"Suit yourself," Jib said, disappearing as suddenly as he had appeared.

Blase smiled at me. "Jib," he said. "What a nut.

39

You have to forgive him—you know, old money, big trust fund, private school in Switzerland."

And here I'd always thought it was the *underprivileged* for whom you were supposed to make allowances.

"Sort of eccentric, but also a genius. He's a hell of a writer and something of a Renaissance man: he paints, flies twin-engine Cessnas, collects baseball cards and plays a fair cello."

"Sounds busy."

Hank Williams was singing, slowly, mournfully, and Blase and I fell silent, sipped our beers, and scratched at the soggy labels.

Barley malt, hops, yeast. Ingredients jointly sufficient for fermentation, the cultivation of bacteria and fungi. Decay. Rotting foodstuffs. Funny how some people would give up everything for garbage.

I thought about my parents, still stunned and reeling from their divorce. Like Turks and Armenians, they never got along; as far back as I could remember, they were always busy getting loaded, then hurling food, china, drinks, punches, and insults at each other, with very little time left over to throw things at us kids. But for some reason I was struck to the heart when they casually informed me, by telephone, on a Sunday—the day meant for long-distance chitchat, nothing serious, just simple summaries of recent events, a brief exchange of love-you-miss-yous—that they were finally calling it quits. I felt nostalgic for my childhood, the one I didn't have, filled with jolly family picnics and snowy, cozy evenings by the fire playing board games with my sisters, my parents snuggled up on the couch, reading. Then I thought of Mark, my last real boyfriend, and the string of bounty hunters who had singly proclaimed endless love and devotion to my body and mind and jointly consumed nearly all of my modest trust fund. Just as I was deciding what to mourn next—my underachievement at prep school, my frustration with analytic philosophy, or my thighs—Blase said, "So what say we quit this grave-yard and venture into the night, see who's who and what's what where?" I told him I was exhausted; I told him I'd hardly slept last night.

"Know how you feel. I often have that problem myself." *Hayek.* But he actually looked disappointed. Then the brows rose and he said, "Have you consid-ered a hair of the dog? I often find that's just what's needed at moments like this."

"I was *working* all night."

"So a break is what you need. 'All work and no play' and so forth."

"Thanks anyway."

"Well, then, I guess I'm off," he said, rising from the couch.

I nodded.

"What's your name again?" he said.

"Toby Dodge."

"Have you published anything? Should I know you?"

"Definitely not."

Blase leaned toward me, braced himself with his hand against the back of the couch, defining a small space containing only the two of us, like men do when they're coming on to you, and said, "I'm so glad you don't sell insurance." He moved his face closer to

41

mine, looked into my eyes and sent a small current down my spine.

"Hope to see you soon," he said.

"Well, what'd you think of Blase?" David had his arm around my shoulders and he was leaning down, pressing his cheek to mine.

"I think he's an idiot," I said. Then I blabbed on mercilessly about his braggadocio, his chauvinism, his arrogance, his name-dropping, his vaingloriousness, his ridiculous laugh, his awkward perpetual motion, his sneaky, promiscuous drug use, and his playing to the gallery.

David smiled.

Next day, Sunday, I spent four hours trying to construct a cogent, or at least valid, argument for a minor conclusion I needed to support an unsurprising thesis which would help me establish a commonsense view of identity, best put by Bishop Butler: "Everything is what it is and not another thing." Who would have ever thought you'd have to argue for *that*?

Every time I felt I had made a little progress, dug a little deeper, unearthed a minor artifact from the metaphysical terrain, a cold shadow would fall across my work and I'd hear a voice in my head: "But is *that* how we use the word?" It was Wittgenstein, Ludwig Wittgenstein, that twentieth-century philosophical tyrant who, despite the fact that he was dead and buried, kept a firm grip around the throat of philosophy, threatening to choke the life out of it. Before your eyes he would render illusory the meaningfulness of the terms that had lured most, had certainly lured me, into the field: Truth, Beauty, Knowledge, Essence. He would reduce meaning to use, use to practice, and practice he would cash out in terms of form of life—which is to say that like an evil genius with his finger on the button, he might lay to waste all that man had so carefully constructed in the course of the last 2,500 years. Metaphysics would become Grammar. Meaning would become meaninglessness. And wisdom would consist in accepting this.

After four hours of running in place, trying to battle this behemoth with my flawed little argument, I temporarily yielded and began working on cartoons instead. For a few months now, I'd been doing a fashion series I called "Animal Apparel," with cartoons like this:

Chapeaux

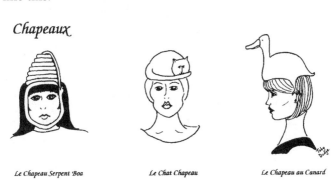

Le Chapeau Serpent Boa   *Le Chat Chapeau*   *Le Chapeau au Canard*

I had secret hopes of getting my cartoons published one day, if not in the *Manhattanite*, where they would be called "drawings," then maybe in the unruly upstart, that provocative little tramp, *New Manhattan*.

* * *

At around six I was busy spying on my parents, who occupied the apartment across from mine in the building next door—of course, they weren't really my parents, but that's how I thought of this couple since they were both major league pitchers, and very imaginative in what they found pitchable: potted plants, dumbbells, small furniture, even a TV set. The woman appeared to be attractive and refined in a gourmet-potato-chip way, while the husband was the white T-shirt, outta-my-face type. Clearly it was a you-say-potato I-say-spud relationship; it would never work.

The woman was shaking her head, waving her arms like windshield wipers that meet in the middle, when David phoned, asked if I'd like to drop by for a cold one and maybe a game of chess.

I told him sure and dashed back to the window.

Apparently the woman had taken a pot of spaghetti in the fuel tank, but she was okay. I could tell because she was charging her dearly beloved with a broom.

When he answered the door, David gave me a big hug, then stepped back, and I saw him, Blase, rising from the couch.

"What are *you* doing here?" I almost said.

"Hey, Toby," he said, like we were some kind of friends or something. "Nice shirt."

"Thanks."

David moseyed off to the kitchen for beer and Blase settled back into the couch, rested an ankle on a knee, and began bouncing a foot in the air.

"Y'gotta love New York," Blase said.

"Why?"

"It's a twenty-four-hour sideshow and they don't even charge admission. For example, I'm on my way here, minding my own business, and at the corner of Thirty-fourth and Fifth I see this old lady wearing men's briefs over pantyhose—big briefs, I mean they come up to her ribs. I'm talking Baby Huey briefs." Blase hayekked. "Anyway, she's got black rubbers on and a hunting vest over a T-shirt and she's wearing a blue-tinseled rock and roll wig. (*Hayek.*) But here's the kicker: the woman's holding a sign that says, 'To hell with Mrs. Batterby and her flowers!' "

"Her flowers too?"

"You bet," Blase said. "And she's screaming, 'Fuck me! Fuck me! Fuck me!' " Blase did the "Fuck me"'s in a shrill falsetto. Snap. Loud laughing. Some lurching of the torso.

I wanted to slap him because, for some reason, I felt like he was partially responsible for her suffering.

Strange, sometimes it's as if I have thoughts that are solid and lasting, ones I rest on securely or lob at people in an argument. And sometimes I have thoughts like this one, that Blase was somewhat to blame, thoughts that are *feelings*, that suddenly overwhelm me, not with the backing of reason and the weight of conviction, but with an emphatic and compelling spur to action. Thoughts that prompt me to do things I would later regret, like suddenly screaming in a quiet theater, or touching spun-glass insulation, or tasting paint.

Feeling vaguely guilty, I said, "That's pretty funny," and forced a smile.

Blase laughed a little more. Cleared his throat. "That really is a nice shirt," he said.

"Thanks."

Blase began to search his pockets and suddenly said, "Know who you remind me of?"

"Who?"

"Grace Kelly."

"Has she got a nice shirt too?"

"I mean the way you look, your mannerisms."

I was annoyed at Blase for handing me such transparent flattery and annoyed at myself for feeling flattered.

From the inside pocket of his jacket Blase removed a ticket-sized envelope.

"Got a mirror?" he yelled to David.

With a round mirror in one hand and three beers gripped in the other, David sauntered back into the living room, singing "Crazy." While David fussed with the stereo, Blase sprinkled some coke into a tiny pile on the mirror, then handed me a credit card.

"Be my guest," he said, as if making me chop it into lines was doing me a favor.

"No thanks."

Blase began to roll a fifty into a tube.

(Blase would later tell me that one very important rule governing the practice of cocaine consumption was to use the largest bill you had as a tooter. Sometimes he'd rush off to the bank before it closed, not because he needed the cash but because he had to have a Hamilton for the night. Another important rule, equipment-wise, was if you were going to chop it with a credit card, it was better if it was American Express, best if it was gold. And "It's like this," he would tell me. "Unattractive women, and men beneath your station socially or financially, do not like cocaine and would consider it an insult to be offered any. Cocaine is like exercise for the attractive and wealthy, it is *good* for them, but only a lot of overpriced liquids from France or Russia can replenish their precious bodily fluids. And—this is really important—*never* do your own cocaine if you can do that of another. Other people like to share their cocaine, it makes them feel good. Yours should be saved for those who might be able to do you a favor.")

While Blase rolled the Grant into a tube, David was singing along with Patsy Cline, who was singing "Sweet Dreams," and I was arguing with myself: Yes. No. Go. Stay. Warm bed, good night's rest. Haven't hung out with David in ages. Stupid. Fun. Just a little bit. Coke doesn't come in little bits. Then Blase handed me the bill and I snorted up a line.

"Please, have another," he said, as if he were just a grandma with a plate of cookies.

I knew it was time to leave when I was sweating and clenching my jaw so tightly I thought my teeth would shatter, sniffing tingly mucus in that wide-open way, feeling like I could see every object in the room at once, and actually finding Blase charming and attractive.

David thanked me for stopping by and I knew I

was obliged to thank Blase for ushering me into this wretched state, so I did.

When I returned to my apartment at four A.M., my living room/dining room/kitchen seemed foreign, a replica of that room, full of strange smells and too brightly lit, like a room in a hospital. My work sat innocently just where I'd left it, but now it was pulsing with silent reproach.

Lying in bed, I was hollow: a vast, grey nothing in my skull, the marrow drained from my bones, my soul yanked out by its root; I was simply a cold, quivering exoskeleton shed by the real me somewhere in the night. *That's* when I remembered: oh, yeah, I don't like cocaine.

There were three things I didn't like about cocaine. First, it made me feel miserable; second, it always made me forget that it made me feel miserable. Though Blase said it made him feel charming and powerful and elated, quite honestly, cocaine always took from me my sense of well-being and stability and gave me only one thing in return: the desire for more, and this was the third thing I really didn't like about cocaine.

THREE

The Romantic Egoist

Monday afternoon I was carving the word *essence* in one of the four desks in the office of Philosophy Graduate Fellows, thinking in general about the necessary and sufficient conditions for the persistence of an object over time and specifically about whether Romeo and Juliet could survive fusion, while pretending to listen to Della Kramer as she rambled on about some sort of Being-of as opposed to Being-for. Suddenly a zitty boy in a Red Sox cap bum-firsted into the office, yelling, "All right! All right!" to someone in the hall and carrying a bouquet of flowers. Holding the vase with two hands, arms outstretched as if he didn't want to be associated with it, he said, "Flowahs."

Della sprang from her desk, clapping her hands. "Oh, cool! Harry's a total romantic. This is awesome, man."

As she hurried back to her desk with the vase, the boy sucked a corner of his mouth into his cheek and said, "I'll give *you* a tip: *Tip*."

"Just *look* at these, Toby! Sweetheart roses and

fuchsia and tulips and—far out! Alstromeria! He *knows* I love alstromeria!"

When Della removed the little card from the envelope, she looked like someone had just taken an ax to her heart.

"It's for *you*," she said, reluctantly handing over the card.

In a messy, loopy scrawl, it read:

When I walked by this flower shop, I found myself thinking of you, Toby. How about dinner tonight? I'll phone you at home, around six.

Cheers!
Blase

"I thought you said you weren't *seeing* anyone," Della said, as if otherwise the flowers would have been for her.

"I'm not," I said. "It's just a guy I know." I was delighted that someone had sent me flowers, shocked and suspicious that *Blase* had sent me flowers, but oddly charmed that he had used my name.

From my purse I removed the long memo pad and wrote, "Shower on return" underneath "Get dry cleaning." The front section of the pad was devoted to lists about work: a list of questionable rules of inference, a list of premises to refine, a list of books to read, a list of articles to copy, a four-page list of questions like, "What is the Paradox of Analysis?", "Does antiessentialism entail antirealism?", and "What about *haecceities*?" The last section of the book contained practical lists: a list of today's errands, a list of movies to see, garments to mend, and a running list of the people I owed letters to. On my refrigerator at home, I had a list of my character defects (too rigid, too dogmatic about work, not assertive enough in the real world) and a list of my goals for the future, which was simply a list of virtues: wisdom, kindness, courage. My life was so full of lists that I even had lists about making lists: "Make xerox list," "Make new errand list," etc. It was as if once I had inscribed the words on paper, I couldn't *but* do the things written there, as surely as the conclusion tumbles out of the premises of a valid argument, and I couldn't fail to have an orderly, reasonable life.

Blase buzzed my apartment at seven forty-five armed with a single rose and we taxied to a dingy Indian restaurant downtown, a hole-in-the-wall with red carpet and red dimpled candle jars and a ceiling so low it made my hair spark.

Blase slid a chair from under the table, gestured for me to sit, and I admired his chivalry, though we had a little difficulty coordinating his pushing-in motion with my up-and-down motion.

"Would you like me to order?" Blase said. "I know the menu pretty well."

"Sure," I said. *He knew the menu pretty well.* That meant that I'd been brought to one of his standard courting spots, that the maître d' had probably slipped him a knowing wink when he seated us, that this was most likely his usual table.

"I used to come here all the time with Jib," Blase said. "You remember Jib," he assured me.

"I do?"

"He was at David's party. Tall, dark hair—you remember."

"The one in the cocaine T-shirt?"

"Nah, Jib's strictly the button-down-and-blazer type. Anyway, the guy's brilliant, a first-class thinker, a great writer, a regular laff riot. My best friend. A few years ago I lived across the street and we ate here all the time." Blase pinched his nostrils together. "Now that was a great apartment. Two bedrooms, study, sky lights, two full baths, working fireplace, and only six hundred a month."

"Why'd you move?"

"You had to have pets there."

"Had to?"

"Yeah, about four thousand cockroaches, which I really didn't mind till they began eating all my drugs." *Hayek.* "I was going broke supporting their habits and, much worse, I was finding myself alarmingly sober most Saturday nights, a wretched condition for the noble savage. Naturally, I broke my lease and moved out."

Snap. *Hayek.*

I wanted to ask him about coke—did he do it often?—but I wasn't very good at anything that might seem confrontational, outside of philosophy.

In my family, if anything at all distressing occurred (like when my sister Anne got a bad report card, or when Iz fell off the roof, or the time I knocked over a fifth of gin) this is how it would be handled: it would always happen during the cocktail hour, which began early and cloned itself into a whole night, and

Mom would see one of us come scrambling into the kitchen spouting tears with a silent-screaming face, and she'd comfort us with, "I don't want to hear about it." Then if you turned to Dad, looking for comfort or concern, trying to force out words, he'd raise a hand. "Shut up," he'd explain, adding, "And get out," for clarification.

Sometimes, if you persisted in being so annoying, Mom would be a little trigger-happy and you'd get a backhand, which meant her three-karat in the face, which meant a bloody nose. And as you stood there howling with a little red beginning to trickle out of a nostril, and then you realized blood was involved and you could make a *real* scene, Mom would hug you and look accusingly at her hand and say, "This goddamned ring." Later, it was also the goddamned gin, or my goddamned father, or *her* goddamned father, until she finally settled on "if it weren't for you kids." Once she passed through menopause, however, Mom mellowed out quite a lot, gave up the backhand (really she had no choice since we were all taller than she and you can't clobber someone long-distance, or so it seemed to me then) and took to blaming everything on religion.

Blase would later insist I was very insecure and too polite, because I was always thanking everyone, even if it was just a bum accepting my change or a smoker returning my lighter. But it wasn't extreme politeness or insecurity that made me act this way: it was the fear that you could never be sure what would happen if you slipped up somehow, crossed someone. Human behavior was largely unpredictable, I thought,

53

which was why I didn't believe there could really be a science of the mind, which was why I studied logic and good old-fashioned metaphysics, orderly, reasonable areas of inquiry with sound, sensible results.

Blase and I drank beer and told each other the stories of our lives—happy childhoods, happy school days, lots of happy pals—in short, stories of lives no one has ever really lived, stories reserved for strangers, prospective employers, and other people you want to impress, to assure them of the likelihood of a healthy emotional balance and to establish your charm and desirability.

"What do you do in your free time?" I asked.

"Drugs," he said and laughed. "I'm kidding. Actually, aside from photography and philately—that's stamp collecting, to you—don't laugh, but I'm a pretty decent figure skater."

"Really? Not hockey?"

"Nah. I try to stick with the low-risk sports, brain-trauma-wise, which I feel are generally distinguished by their lack of equipment. You know, swimming, running—"

"Cliff diving," I added.

Blase struck me as almost calm: his face and voice seemed soft and relaxed, his laughter was contagious, and he wasn't about to fling himself from his chair, though he did shred his napkin to ribbons, weave it between the tines of his fork, then stab it into what was left of the lamb vindaloo.

"Do you smoke?" he asked.

"No. You?"

"No," he said, adding, "Should I get some cigarettes?"

"Sure," I said.

He lit my cigarette while looking into my eyes, just like a leading man in the movies except he burned himself. But he was pretty suave about pretending to pick up bits of his napkin from the floor so he could stick his fingers in his mouth.

"So you're writing about personal identity," he said.

"That's right."

"Can't say I know much about the issue," he said. "I don't s'pose it has anything to do with birth certificates or drivers' licenses."

I smiled. "You don't s'pose right."

"Wanna brief me on it?"

"Seriously?" I said.

"Yeah," Blase said. "Inquiring minds want to know."

"OK, here's one question," I said. "Suppose there's this guy, call him Fred, who's a real sports fanatic—devours all the sports magazines, is glued to the TV every night, you know. S'pose Fred is also something of a genius—"

"Highly unlikely, given the first assumption," Blase interjected.

"—and let's say he's also enormously kind and gentle. Now, imagine one morning Fred wakes and he's totally changed—he has no interest in sports, he's a complete dunce—can't understand the most basic things—and, moreover, he's cruel and violent. I'm imagining we have here *the same body, same hu-*

man being, but the question is, Is it the same person?
Is it *Fred*?"

"Clearly not," Blase said.

"So this suggests that our concept of a person isn't
the same as our concept of a human being, right?"

"Right," Blase said.

"But couldn't we also think about it like this:
Fred's undergone a profound change—like Gregor in
Metamorphosis. 'He's so different now!' his wife says.
'He never used to be like this.' Notice, *'he*'s' different—implies *he*'s still in the picture, right? What's so
bothersome is that there are ways to fill this out that
might make us lean toward one or another view: if the
guy who wakes up seems to remember doing and
thinking everything the guy who went to bed the night
before seemed to remember doing and thinking, we'd
probably want to say it *is* the same guy, right? Especially if *he* noticed the change in his character. Or
s'pose the change was *gradual*, took place over the
course of twenty years—his interest in sports gradually weakens, he slowly grows violent, etc."

"So what do you make of this?"

"I think our concept of a person is tied closely
to our concept of a human being, but that it essentially involves behavioral patterns, dispositions to act
in certain ways, whereas our concept of human being doesn't. Our concept of a person seems to be
pragmatic—people's dispositions change, constantly,
without our ever wondering, 'Is it the same person?',
like when someone begins or ends a habit, say someone quits smoking. It's only when a core of what we

consider to be basic dispositions changes that the question of whether it's the same person arises."

"Which means?"

"I think 'person' isn't really a fundamental concept, it doesn't reach out into the world and point to a real thing."

"You mean there are no people?" Blase was laughing.

"In the strict and philosophical sense, no." I was astounded at myself, and then I heard Wittgenstein:

When philosophers use a word—"knowledge," "being," "object," "I," "proposition," "name"— and try to grasp the essence of the thing, one must always ask oneself: is the word ever actually used in this way in the language-game which is its original home?

Blase shook his head, smiling. "Philosophers say the darnedest things."

I smiled weakly.

A philosophical problem has the form: "I don't know my way about."

"Why did you decide to go into philosophy?" Blase said.

I considered. "Maybe because it was so *hard*."

"God, you really are Protestant, aren't you?"

I remembered my dad when my first report card arrived from Harvard. I'd already decided to major in mathematics and got an A− in calculus. "An A-minus?" Dad said. "What happened? Why didn't you get the A?" The next semester, I got the A in calculus II: "Not bad," Dad said, "but not an A-plus, is it?" Finally, in second-year calculus, I got the A+ and Dad said, "Yeah, but it was *easy*, wasn't it?" When I began philosophy and stopped bringing home As, Dad simply questioned my choice of fields and in such a way that revealed his ignorance about the nature of value, that showed he didn't understand intrinsic value, could only view something as valuable if it was a means to something else. "Philosophy? Now what are you gonna do with *that*?"

"Your parents must be pretty proud of you," Blase said, "having this fancy fellowship at NYU and all."

"I'm not sure 'proud' is the word," I said.

I asked whether he enjoyed being at Columbia. "Pretty impressive teaching job."

"Oh, it's okay," Blase said. "Like any other teaching job, I'm sure."

We talked on relentlessly, cheerfully inventing our New Best Selves, through the shrimp malai and the ginger ice cream and well into our fourth beers. We had similar backgrounds—old New Englanders, lapsed Protestants (which we agreed was probably redundant), horseback-riding preppies, Ivy Leaguers—similar tastes in books, films, and music, a profound love of mangos, Alfred Hitchcock, and Bugs Bunny, and the same dream: to live on the coast with lots of land, gardens, a sheepdog chasing happy children through a meadow, plenty of travel. We talked on urgently, as if something were at stake, as if we were approaching a moment when a decision would be made, as if this evening provided our one chance and when it came to end, something would be forever lost or forever ours.

When the Punjabi waiter kindly informed us to "get out now, please," Blase said, "Would you like to get a bottle of wine, motor uptown, and check out who's floating down the East River?"

When we reached a bench off Beekman Place, Blase removed from his jacket two glasses he'd swiped from the restaurant.

"We don't have a corkscrew," I said, and Blase said, "No problem," and began to tap the bottom of the wine bottle against the back of the bench.

I smiled as he tapped.

"It's coming," he said, tapping harder.

I smiled some more.

He wrinkled his nose and pulled his lips tight across his teeth as if he might scare the cork out of the bottle. Tap, tap, tap.

"Looks like it's really in there," I said.

Blase said, "Now, just a few light taps on the side . . . " and brought the neck of the bottle down on the bench and it broke off, leaving a rim of jagged spikes.

"There," he said.

Blase generously filled the glasses and we raised them and he cleared his throat and said:

> "Give me women, wine and snuff
> Until I cry out 'hold, enough!' "

"Just kidding," he said, and touched my arm and hayekked and I sort of smiled. He raised his glass again, I raised mine, and this time he said:

> "There's a sigh for yes, and a sigh for no,
> And a sigh for I can't bear it!
> O what can be done, shall we stay or run?
> O cut the sweet apple and share it!"

"Keats," he said, and he kissed me and we clinked glasses. We gazed out at the river, the woolly reflection of lights in the water.

After we finished our second glass, Blase raised the broken bottle and said, "I have made an important discovery."

"What's that?"

"Alcohol, when taken in sufficient quantities, produces all the effects of intoxication."

I felt like I'd heard it before, but it was still funny so I laughed and he laughed and we fell silent. I stared into my glass, watched the wine slip down the sides.

Then I told Blase about my parents' divorce and started weeping, which was unfortunate because, as I've already mentioned, I'm no Helen when it comes to the waterworks. (As my sister Isabelle so sensitively puts it, when I cry, my eyes narrow and my upper lip swells and comes to a point in the center and I look like a duck.) It keeps some people from having much sympathy for me at such moments (Isabelle actually

60

bursts out laughing), but Blase took me in his arms and rocked me gently and stroked my hair and said, "It's all right. It's all right, sweetheart."

He lifted my head with one finger, looked in my eyes, and said, "I wish I could go back in time and undo the harm that's been done to you," and he kissed me.

After we'd finished the wine, Blase leaned back, crossed his legs, and began kicking the air.

"My father's dead," he suddenly announced.

"I'm sorry," I said.

"Died in a car accident. Last year. Some idiot ran a red light. He didn't even see it coming."

"I'm so sorry."

"My sister was in the car. It left her a total quadriplegic. Can't even feed herself." Blase looked like he was going to cry, but he just sniffled.

Here, then, was the explanation for his snorting cocaine and acting like such a jackass at David's: He was grieving. He was desperately trying to numb his excruciating pain.

"I guess we've both had our share of tragedy," he said, and I nodded, but I felt like a fraud. So my parents got a divorce. So what? Big deal. Happens every day.

(Five weeks later, when we were engaged, Blase confessed that he'd been exaggerating that night: his father *had* been in a car crash, but that was years ago and, really—thank God—he was fine; he was dying to meet me, wanted us to come up the next weekend. As for his sister, well, he was an only child—but he'd always *wanted* a sister. First, he said he made it up because he figured if I thought he'd endured major anguish, too, then I'd feel closer to him, like there was something profound we shared. Then he said he'd done it for *me*: he wanted me to feel better and to help me put my parents' divorce in perspective. "And it worked, didn't it?" he said.)

As we strolled around Beekman Place, sizing up the brownstones and single-family residences as if we were actually considering purchasing one, saying things like: "I'd never live there" or "I love those windows," I heard myself asking, "Do you have any children?"

Almost my entire life I had been repulsed by human neonates—those doughy, muggy, cranky, croupy, stinky, wriggling larvae with raw, rashy cheeks and scabby, bald heads who always insisted on sitting near me on airplanes, in restaurants, or at the movies so they could break my eardrums and push me to the brink of madness with their otherwise superfluous, relentless shrieking and wailing. Actually, babies had completely unnerved me—they seemed so powerful, effortlessly compelling grown men and women to make fools of themselves: to babble like idiots in a singsong soprano; to crawl around on all fours, bucking and snorting and braying like jackasses; and to give up liquor and eat balanced meals and take up jogging and stay home nights. When I'd see one leading a woman by the hand or forcing her to assume the position of Nubian slave toting the Master in her arms or propelling him in a perambulator up the avenue, I would hightail it the other way.

After a lifetime of such fear of *infantes sub specie*

(hominum sapientum), I was caught unawares one day when I suddenly found myself in line at the grocery store staring at one, bubbling and gurgling incoherently and grinning like a drunk, wanting to stroke her cheek with my finger, to pick her up and squeeze her mushy body.

"No. God, no," Blase said. Then he added, "Though I'd like to, someday."

"Me too," I said.

When he brought me to the steps of my building, Blase stuffed his hands in his pockets and began kicking at a crack in the cement.

"This was great," he said.

I smiled.

We watched his foot kick at the crack, then Blase took a step toward me. He looked at me with those shiny grey child-eyes.

"I love your hair," he said. "Your nose." *My nose.* People could mention clothes or teeth or your earrings, and it might not mean anything at all. But when they started talking noses, you knew it was serious.

Blase stared at my mouth.

He moved closer, crossing some boundary, which made me shiver. When he held me, began to whisper in my hair, I suddenly knew the limits of my body, the soft smell of his skin.

He held me closer, whispered something that sounded like "water rat dove."

And I felt small and lovely and his.

FOUR

A Diamond as Big as the Ritz

Have you ever noticed that many stores have electronic entrance doors and manual exits? It's as if they're delighted with you at first, can't wait to usher you in: "Hi! Glad to see ya! Here, allow me." But while you're busy inside—not shoplifting or reading the magazines or breaking the protective seals on products you want to sniff, but behaving yourself, doing all the things you believe you're supposed to do in a store—they undergo a change of heart, and when it's time for you to leave, the doors rest heavily on their hinges—"Push or pull? Figure it out yourself!"—and slam "Good riddance!" behind you. Well, that pretty much sums up Blase's behavior at the beginning and end of our relationship.

The next six weeks were, perhaps, ho-hum in the life of Princess Grace, but unheard of in real life, at least in my life. Flowers arrived daily at the Fellows office for me, making a real enemy out of Della Kramer until she'd ridden Harry hard enough so one day he sent her a cone of blue daisies.

"You know what daisies stand for, don't you?" Della said, cradling the bouquet like a baby. "Honesty, optimism, and generosity. And blue. Blue is for purity, eternity, and enchantment." She smiled at the bouquet like she expected it to smile back. "Harry's very deep," she added, implying, of course, that Blase was very shallow.

Blase sent telegrams to my office: "Urgent. Thinking of you," they might say, or "Who's on your dance card tonight? Could it be me?" He dedicated songs and sent messages to me via the radio station we played in the office, songs like "Let's Do It" and "Ain't She Sweet?" When I arrived home at the end of the day, there would often be a basket of tropical fruit or roses waiting for me on the front hall table, and inside my mailbox I'd usually find something from Blase: a photograph he'd had made into a postcard of us in an open carriage; a necklace with four pearls strung on a gold chain, one for each week we'd been together, he said; a greeting card containing a fistful of glitter that fell, sparkling, to my feet, and written inside, "Here is my heart."

Blase courted me everywhere. He courted me uptown. He courted me downtown. He courted me in the subway, in taxis, on sidewalks, in elevators, in Central Park, on the steps of St. Patrick's, at the Oyster Bar, the theater, at the MOMA, the Frick and the Met, at Rockefeller Center, in the Gotham Book Mart, in cozy Second Avenue piano bars, at the Box Tree, Harry's Bar, the Old Town, and the Lion's Head— by phone, by singing telegram, on roller skates, with his mouth full.

Then he rented a limo and brought me to the Plaza for the night.

"Why don't you take a dive in that fountain?" Blase said, gesturing, and I could see he wasn't kidding.

"Why would I want to do that?"

"You know. Zelda," he said.

Well, I didn't know Zelda. All I knew was that I'd spent an hour and a half getting ready and my dress had a Dry Clean Only label.

"Scott Fitzgerald's wife," Blase added.

Oh, *that* Zelda, I thought, but I still didn't know her. All I knew was that she and F. were said to be a wild couple and he wrote *The Great Gatsby* and everyone thought he was overrated these days. I took a dive on our king-size bed instead.

"Can we order room service?" I said.

"Of course," Blase said, and kissed me. I almost fainted when I saw the prices. "Fifteen dollars for ice?" I said. "Forget it. Let's go find a deli." But Blase insisted that it was probably Evian ice and even if it wasn't, I was worth it. "Yes, but is *the ice* worth it?" I said, and he shut me up with his very soft mouth.

"He's really taken with you," my best friend Claire said. We were sitting in Grassroots, splitting a pitcher.

I smiled. "I guess I'm kind of taken with him."

"What happened to 'Oh, Claire! I met the *biggest jerk* last night!' Remember that?"

I laughed and shook my head. "Never trust your first impression."

"Yeah," Claire said, "but don't forget it either."

*   *   *

Blase and I talked about everything: our parents and what we knew of their parents and their parents, our real childhoods, our small triumphs (mine: mastering the art of French cooking; Blase's: winning the National Junior Spelling Bee in the sixth grade), our deepest fears (mine: that the order I'd established in my life was so fragile that if I ever let go of the rudder, turned away for a moment, all would be reduced to chaos; Blase's: that good taste would go out of style or Brooks Brothers would go out of business—*hayek*— "no, seriously, I fear dying wretched and destitute and in obscurity"). We talked about turning points in our lives, our first loves, the fictional characters we most identified with (I said Thumbelina; Blase said Jay Gatsby). Blase heard my fears, regrets, and resentments.

"It must have been really hard having alcoholic parents," he said.

"*My* parents?" I was shocked. "Alcoholic?"

"Heavy drinkers, then," he said. "Whatever you're comfortable calling them. It sounds like things were pretty turbulent, pretty unpredictable."

"Pretty crazy," I said.

He held me, rocked me slowly, said, "That's all behind you now."

We discussed astrology, ESP, after-death experiences, free will, bad faith, and God. We talked about heaven and hell and the problem of evil.

"I used to think that all the evil and suffering in the world proves there isn't a God," Blase said.

"What changed your mind?"

"I found myself believing in God anyway so I knew the proof had to be flawed. I guess it's like they say, one man's modus ponens is another man's modus tollens."

"But do you really want to endorse this form of reasoning: 'I see reasons for not-p. I don't see reasons for p. But I believe that p. Therefore, p'?"

"Hey, we do it all the time," Blase said. "Shoot, *you* do it all the time."

"*I* do?"

"Yeah, it's called wishful thinking."

Blase had been raised as a "high Episcopalian," he said, faithfully attending Sunday school and church and so forth.

"Maybe it's just my upbringing, but I think there's *something*," he said. "Something larger than us, something whose principles in some way govern us."

"You mean something other than the whole of the universe, the laws of nature?"

"Yeah," he said. "Something intelligent."

"Don't tell my mother," I said. Then I informed him that my mother was inordinately suspicious of religion, took an immediate dislike of anyone pledging allegiance to one, or to a Higher Power, and explained people she didn't like or understand—which included everyone not exactly like her, which included everyone—in terms of religion. "What did you expect?" she'd said when my last boyfriend dumped me for a lovely, lithe, compact little bitch of a karate instructor. "He's Lutheran-after-all." The balding old woman down the street was rich because she was Jewish-of-course. On the other hand, the Kleinfelters in Mar-

blehead went bankrupt because *they* were Jewish-
you-see. Any quality, any behavior of anyone at
all (excepting Mom herself) was entirely explicable by
their religion. Mom was exempt, I think, because she
was agnostic, and question marks can't explain anything.

"Say no more, say no more," Blase said. "I can
charm the leeriest of matriarchs."

It seemed no territory was off limits, we could talk
about anything: our failures and fears as well as our
hopes and dreams. And, unlike my last real boyfriend,
a painter with an anti-intellectual bent who resented
what he called "the tyranny of logic in Western
thought" and argued that "free and aesthetic thinking," the kind induced by drugs and alcohol and the
relentless intoning of mystical mantras, was the way
to Truth and threw his beer can at me when I pointed
out that the standard he was trying to attack was the
very standard he was using to mount the attack—unlike him, Blase had a deep respect for rigor and a
child's curiosity about the most fundamental questions. He prodded me into discussing the ontological
status of numbers, set theory, the infinite, and listened
carefully while I presented Cantor's diagonal proof of
two nonequivalent infinite sets. When I'd finished, he
said, "Good Lord! One infinite greater than another?
I see it, but I don't believe it." He seemed to take a
special interest in my thesis, to think about it when we
were apart, later raising questions, smart questions,
some of which went right to the heart of the issue.

"Do you *really* think there are no people?"

"On Tuesdays and Thursdays. Mondays, Wednesdays, and Fridays, I think there are people in the same way that there are corporations or clubs."

"Do you think there are corporations and clubs?"

"Not *really*," I said, as if I were saying something over and above no.

Blase smiled and shook his head.

Ours was the sort of courtship I'd sort of dreamed of as a teenager. But then, it was the early seventies, and women were supposed to be men, so my dream was the weak-kneed dream of a traitor. To be a woman, or to be treated like one, was, for some reason, to be degraded in those days. We burned our bras and wore sweatshirts and jeans and no makeup, and even though I believed in equal rights and peace signs and so forth, I secretly longed for miniskirts and go-go boots, false eyelashes and wearing my hair in a flip. I'd given up on the women's movement when it began the urgent, critical debates about whether women were postpersons, postalcarriers, postalenvoys, postalemissaries, postalambassadors, postaldispatchers—but not, God forbid, post*women*. I thought, to hell with it, we're still underpaid. Perhaps, ironically, something gained by the death of the women's movement was that it was no longer demeaning to be a woman or to be called a woman. We could admit it: No, we do not have penises. And yes, it's okay for men to pay the restaurant tab or hold a heavy door—if they earn better wages and are physically stronger (which, in general, they do and they are). I thought, Why is this acknowledgment of, and temporary compensation for, the way things are equivalent to acceptance? Things can be changed; for now, a balancing out of inequalities struck me as just and polite. And besides, I'd always wanted to wear high heels, seamed stockings, push-up bras, and corsets.

We were in love. We were madly in love. We read Donne and Yeats and Shakespearean sonnets. We shared a toothbrush and traded chewing gum. We made up love poems and love songs and love names for each other. New York was suddenly new, suddenly beautiful, and suddenly ours. Everyone said we went together like peaches and cream, prince and princess, Mickey and Minnie, eggs and b.

All the things that had initially bugged me about Blase—his boasting, his chauvinism, the snap—had vanished. His laugh became funny and infectious. His movements seemed interesting, charming, even his genuine bowlegged walk. And as far as I could tell, he didn't do coke anymore.

Almost from the very beginning, a strange phenomenon began to occur. While Blase was insisting we should be Scott and Zelda (which I said was fine with me as long as I got to be Scott), other people were insisting we were brother and sister. In stores and restaurants, if Blase had scooted off to the men's, clerks and waitresses (waitpersons, whatever) would ask me, "Do you think your brother would like this?" or "Would your brother care for another that?" At first, we found it hilarious—"Ha, ha, ha. Let's kiss and give them the willies"—but then it became very unsettling, at least to me. When we would have drinks with distant friends of his family, or mere acquaintances of Blase's, people would glance at me, do a double take, and sometimes even gasp, like I had some exotic species of insect crawling out of my eyes, and say, "Blase! I didn't know you had a *sister*!" When we met Blase's childhood nanny for lunch, she actually fainted, then recovered herself for a moment and said, in a strained whisper, "I thought you was young Mrs. Regenhere," and fainted again and had to be carried to a back room of the restaurant to recuperate. It really spooked me, but Blase didn't want to talk about it.

Early on in the relationship, during the time when other new couples learn how to communicate and share feelings, Blase and I were exercising some of the skills we'd acquired in childhood, both of us having been raised to dodge confrontation, to believe that disagreement, not to mention arguing, was a bad thing that inevitably damaged relationships, and that, while the sharing of positive emotion was optional, the negative feelings were powerful and private and deserved to be covered with sand in the kitty box of one's mind. So we got on perfectly. Everybody said so.

One night I phoned my mother to ask if she could spare some money as I was going broke trying to keep up my share of courtship expenses, which consisted of a few cab rides and the occasional round of drinks. My slim stipend had to last seven more months and the balance on my trust fund bore an alarming resemblance to some of my friends' monthly paychecks.

Though my parents had a respectable amount of money, they made it clear that we wouldn't see a penny of it until their deaths. My sister Kate said they set it up this way for tax reasons, but Anne thought my parents intended it to be a consolation to us, since we'd be so sad when they died. "Plus it would also be a reward," she added, "for our having been so good to them throughout their lives." "More like *bribery*," Isabelle said. "To make sure we will have been so good to them throughout their lives." So I didn't have much money on hand, like Blase.

"Hi, Mom. It's Toby."

"Yes, I could tell," she said. "So what about this Blase?"

"How do you know about Blase?"

"I have my ways." Mom loved saying things like that, implying she kept me under constant surveillance, there wasn't anything I could keep from her, so I might as well come clean about all the gritty details of my life.

"He's a man I'm seeing."

"I know *that*. I mean, is he Catholic?"

"What?"

" 'Blase'," she said. "What kind of a name is that? I don't *think* it's Jewish and God knows it's not Protestant. What's his family name?"

"Regenhere."

"How do you spell it?"

"Like it sounds."

"Could be anything," she said. "Sounds Catholic, to me—French Catholic."

"Episcopal," I said. "English Episcopal," I added,

in case there was any other kind. "But he doesn't go to church."

Mom was impressed.

"Did Izzy tell you about him?"

"That's for me to know," she said, just like a little kid.

"Do you think you could send some money?" I said.

"What for?"

"Phone bills."

There was a long pause during which I heard her take two drags from a cigarette. Then I heard her swallow.

"What was that you were saying?"

"I was asking if I could borrow some money. For the phone bill."

"*Borrow* some money, huh. Toby, one thing you'll learn when you're a mother is that children *never* borrow money from their parents—they *steal* it."

"Well, may I please steal some money, then?"

"Why don't you ask your father?"

My father? The man who'd kept a log of what his children owed him for their upbringing, who'd let us drive in death traps and junkers in our teens while he and Mom drove Saabs, who'd constantly accused me and my sisters of bleeding him dry though we had no credit, no checks, and got no allowance? The man who'd followed up, "Your mother and I are getting a divorce" with "I've decided not to spend more than thirty-five dollars on any of you girls for Christmas and birthdays"?

"I don't think so."

"Okay. But first I want you to tell me about this Blase."

"What about him?"

"Is he religious? Sounds Catholic to me."

"Mom, we've been through that."

"Right," she said. "So what do you want for Christmas?"

"It's *October*."

"*I* know that," she said. "Someone *else* wants to know."

"Let me guess: Blase phoned you."

"Sorry, can't say. I promised not to mention anything. By the way, do you like sapphires?"

This was another thing about Mom: she couldn't keep a secret as long as most people keep junk mail. It was as if she believed secrets only had currency while you shared them; if you held on to one for too long, it was sure to come out and lose all value. When she accidentally learned about the suicide of a neighbor's husband, and was sworn to secrecy by the chief of police who felt it his duty to break it to the new widow, Mom hurried over and stood in the woman's front doorway, gaping, until the woman asked, "What is it?" and Mom said, "I was just wondering how you'll fit a wake in here."

Funny, but none of my sisters could really accept the way Mom was either, so we continued confiding in her as if we really expected that she'd keep quiet. Since she and Dad were very serious about drinking, if you phoned one of them after the start of the cocktail hour, you should expect a certain amount of incoherence and forgetfulness, and if you phoned back the next day during the sober hour, you should expect a certain amount of chewing out for never phoning. Still, all of us phoned around seven P.M. and acted as if we'd get a normal mom or dad. I think that's a pretty good definition of insanity: expecting that *this time* things will be different than they've always been in the past.

Mom wanted to know everything about Blase, wouldn't hang up until she'd heard all about his family, his job, his prospects for the future, his educational background, how he was treating me, did we plan a religious wedding, and so forth.

"Mom, there's been no talk of marriage."

"There will be," she said. "Trust me. By the way, are you sure he's not Jewish? He sounds very wealthy."

"I'm sure, Mom."

"Either he's Jewish or he's spending his whole salary on you." This was something that had occurred to me before. Where was he getting all this money? I supposed that Columbia professors were well paid by academic standards, but no one well paid by academic standards was *really* well paid.

"I'll bet his family is loaded," Mom said. "One of those old Presbyterian families that's been squirreling it away for years. I'll bet he has a nice trust."

Halloween, Blase took me to a party at his best friend Jib's. "It'll be great," he said. "You'll get to meet Everybody," which I guess was supposed to be good news, but I actually loathed being the new girlfriend meeting Everybody, which, I think, was something of a contradiction since the boyfriend would always go, "Hey, Everybody! This is Toby," and then he'd add, "Toby, this is Everybody" so I'd still know Nobody.

Blase had talked about Jib from early on—Jib was the greatest person Blase knew; he'd inherited a good deal of money which he spent carelessly on girlfriends and called his "Lust Fund"; Jib was clever; Jib was handsome; Jib had more friends than garbage has flies. Jib was writing a novel, which was bound to be first-rate. Jib was charmed. He never took anything too seriously, could make a good time out of a car accident, saw the possibility for hilarity in a bounced check.

I smiled weakly, said I couldn't wait to meet him, but Blase informed me I already had. "When we met," he said. "At David's party."

"Oh yeah." The guy with the Platonic grudge.

At the Salvation Army I found a grey 1950s working girl's suit, with short jacket and tight knee-length skirt, and a grey pillbox hat that almost matched. I bought fifteen white felt doves at a craft store and a bottle of ketchup. When Blase picked me up that night, he was his usual Brooks Brothers self, while I was wearing the suit and hat with the doves carefully basted all over me like a Central Park statue only I had droplets of ketchup on my face and clothes instead of bird poop.

"What are you supposed to be?"

"Tippi Hedren. In *The Birds*."

He laughed.

"I thought it was going to be a *costume* party."

77

"I'm *sure* it is," Blase said. "I just never wear one, that's all."

"Give me a minute," I said, removing the hat.

"Wait. You're not even thinking of changing, are you?"

"Of course I am."

"Sweetheart, that's a great costume. Really. With these little pigeons—" he said affectionately, fingering the wing of a bird on my forearm.

"Doves," I said.

"Huh?"

"Doves. They should be pigeons but they're doves."

"*Better* than pigeons," Blase said. He kissed the tip of my nose. "And you look beautiful. Don't change."

"But you're not dressed up."

"Everyone else will be, honest."

Jib answered the door in a blue pin-striped shirt and jeans. Apparently he'd decided to go as Blase. Behind him was a scale: on one side, little metal discs, on the other, a pile of coke.

"This is Toby," Blase said.

I felt one of the birds wobble on my hat. I couldn't even look at Jib, cool Jib, funny Jib, brilliant Jib, beloved Jib.

"Hey, is that Valentino?" Jib said. He and Blase cracked up, then Blase put his arm around me and said, "Sweetheart, it's just a *joke*," but I didn't feel consoled because I hadn't known Jib was addressing me.

Everyone else came in preppy costumes: blue

blazers and pin-striped shirts, silk cocktail dresses and pearls. If only I really did look like Tippi Hedren or my gorgeous sister Anne in my *Birds* costume I would have been able to laugh with the people laughing at me. And even though my pantyhose were control-topped, it seemed my stomach led the way to the makeshift bar, where I poured myself a stiff one, then tried to penetrate the boundary of the small circle of people standing to the side of the bar, right next to me: three men and two women shifting their weight, staring at, apparently listening to, the guy in the dark blue suit holding forth about something, so I inched forward, stared too, shifted my weight, and when the guy in the dark blue suit said, "So he said he was from Bronxville!" and heads tossed and everyone laughed, I tossed my head and laughed too, feeling the bird teeter on my hat and the man nearest me said, "Oh, you know Fischer?" and everyone was looking at me with suspended smiles and I shook my head and the smiles faded, making room for the incredibly awkward moment that followed.

"Toby Dodge," I said, extending my hand to the man nearest me, and he took it and nodded and then, without forming any prior intention to do so, I discovered myself making my way around the circle, "Toby Dodge," smiling, shaking everyone's hand like I was running for some office, since I was the only one smiling and no one offered their name. I watched my arm move toward each person, a bird near the elbow and one near a ketchupy wrist. After everyone knew who I was, the man in the dark blue suit cleared his throat and said, "So anyway ... "

I poured another stiff one, then backed into a dark corner from where I watched all the beautiful boys and girls begin to dance and sing along with "Rock the Casbah," which made me feel really uncool, not only because I was standing, hiding, by myself at a party, dressed like a victim, but because I had thought it was "Rob the Cash Box." Blase was still by the door with Jib, laughing and rocking back on his heels—like Santa, as whom I desperately wished he were dressed. I felt like the one kid at the pajama party wearing Dr. Dentons.

The only way you would have known it was a Halloween party was when Jib entered the living room carrying a rectangular tray on which lines of cocaine were chopped up to spell: "HALLOWEEN." I knew I'd just feel worse if I ingested any of it, and when Jib approached me, held the tray out to me, I said, "No thanks," but it came out "Thanks" and I snorted two lines.

Finally Blase bopped over, took my arm, and began towing me across the room, saying, "Come meet some folks." He introduced me to Gina, Brendon, and Johnny, who'd been leaning together, whispering conspiratorially on the couch until we approached. After Blase gave everyone my name, spelling it for them when Gina said, "Toadie?", he added, "Toby's getting her doctorate in philosophy." While Brendon and Johnny simply stared, Gina got to her feet, put her hand on my shoulder, and said, "Philosophy! I love philosophy! Who's your favorite philosopher? Mine's Shirley MacLaine. Didn't you just love *Out on a Limb*?"

"I've never read it."

"You've never read it?" Gina look astounded.

"I'm interested in metaphysics," I said, meaning the science of being qua being and the attributes adhering to it in virtue of its nature.

"But it's all *about* metaphysics," she replied, meaning the unverifiable results of sloppy flights of fancy. "Auras and astral travel and stuff."

"Well, really my area of concentration is personal identity," I said, trying to back away from her.

"Then you've really got to read her other book, too! She writes all about past lives and that Ra—, Ra—, oh, that Peruvian god. You know."

I pardoned myself and as I elbowed through the crowd, trying to knock off a dove, I noticed I was being tailed by a tall woman with short dark hair and a boy's body. When I reached the bathroom, she said, "I'm Cerise. I *love* girly girls."

I didn't know what to make of that until she put her hand on my breast and squeezed it.

"I love *these*," she said, and as I dashed into the bathroom and felt for the lock, she yelled, "Sit on my face and I'll guess your weight."

When I was sure she had gone, I hurried back to the living room and whispered to Blase, who was laughing with two Barbie dolls and a Ken over some marvelous witticism just tossed off by Jib, "Can't we go?"

"Toby," Blase said. "You remember Jib."

"Hi," I said.

Jib nodded, looking off toward the living room, looking this way and that, like a bird, blinking quickly from behind his glasses and sniffling. I said to Blase, again, "Can't we go?"

"Good idea," Jib said. "We've got three limos downstairs waiting to power us to Playland." Playland was New York's club-of-the-month; it had rides and a fun house and games where the prize was a drink.

We all crammed into the limos; Blase got in front with the driver and I sat on his lap. "We'll go back to your place," he said, and kissed my ear.

" 'Right. Percy gets the bird. Let him eat cake. And now to a more urgent matter. While I'm dressing, will you be mixing me a strengthening cocktail?' " Blase and I were cuddled up in my bed and Blase was reading to me from *Jeeves and the Feudal Spirit*.

" 'A strengthening cocktail'," Blase said. "Just what I could use right now. Darling, do we have any strengthening cocktails?"

"Jib doesn't like me, does he?"

"Of course he does. But more importantly, *I* like you. And I like your strengthening cocktails."

"Blase, I'm pretty sure Jib hates me."

"Why do you say that?"

"He hardly said a word to me tonight. He was acting as if I wasn't there. And he's your best friend."

Blase dropped the Wodehouse and held me close, so we were cheek to cheek.

"I don't even think he looked at me."

"Sure he did."

"How do you know?"

"Because he said, 'I'll bet that bird-chick makes supreme strengthening cocktails.'" Blase tickled me and we kissed. Then we were in the kitchen concocting strengthening cocktails.

The following night Blase took me to the Box Tree, an old brownstone on Forty-ninth Street decorated with European antiques, wallpaper, and fresh flowers. We were led upstairs to a private room with a long wooden table, a crackling fire in the fireplace, and a vase of red roses sitting at my place.

"Oh, Blase. This is lovely!" I said.

After Blase toasted me with Yeats's "He Wishes for the Cloths of Heaven," the love poem of a poor man, which seemed somewhat inappropriate, he said, "Well, darling, what will it be?"

"I don't have a menu," I said, and Blase laughed.

"I mean, yes or no."

"Do I love you? Yes."

Blase looked worried. Hadn't I seen *The Daily* today? No, I hadn't; I'd been too busy trying to catch up on all the work I'd let slide. Why? Blase smacked his forehead with his hand.

"I put an ad on the front page—you know, near the index," he said. "I asked you to marry me."

I began to laugh. I couldn't help it.

"Don't laugh; I'm *serious*. Will you marry me?"

I kept laughing, I don't know why.

"Look," Blase said, digging into his jacket pocket. "I even have a ring!" and I lost it. I had to walk around the room and drink some water before my breathing returned to normal and Blase could say, "I have something else for you." He retrieved a book from the fireplace mantel: *The Collected Poems of W. B. Yeats.* On the title page he'd written:

> When you are old and grey and full of sleep,
> And nodding by the fire, take down this book,
> And slowly read, and dream of the soft look
> Your eyes had once, and of their shadows deep;
>
> How many loved your moments of glad grace,
> And loved your beauty with love false or true,
> But one man loves the pilgrim soul in you,
> And loves the beauty of your changing face.

"It's Yeats, of course," Blase said. "I changed it a little." He moved close to me, kissed me, and slipped the ring on my finger. I started to cry.

"Will you? Please?" Blase said.

Blase loved me. I loved him. He respected my work, he respected me. We had similar values, similar goals, the same dream. What more was needed?

"Promise you'll never leave me?" I said.

"Of course!"

"I mean it. I'll never give you a divorce."

"Divorce isn't like that anymore," Blase said. "You just help yourself. But I'll never leave you and I'll never give you cause to leave me."

"Yes," I said. "Yes, yes, yes."

* * *

Later, I looked at the ring and almost choked. Set between two enormous sapphires was a huge, bright diamond, "as big as the Ritz," Blase had said.

"How could you possibly afford this? I can't imagine Columbia professors are *that* well paid."

"Actually," Blase said, "I'm an assistant professor, or rather, I was."

"Huh?"

"I just quit."

"Quit?"

"Well, no. Actually, not *quit*—though I was thinking about it. I mean, I wanted to quit. I was *going* to quit, but they made it easy on me and asked me to leave first."

"That's terrible," I said. "Why?"

"They were jealous of me—my colleagues, I mean. I told them, and I guess I'd better tell you, I've decided to write a biography of Fitzgerald. Blow Mizener and Turnbull out of the water."

"I see," I said, but I didn't. Why would anyone be fired for wanting to write a book? I had thought the supreme dictum of academia was "Publish or perish."

"When did this happen?"

"Two months ago," he said.

"What?"

Blase leaned toward me and held my hands. "Toby, you know I've always wanted to be a writer, but I just can't do it while I'm holding a real job. Can you accept that? Me being a writer? You being a writer's wife?"

"Sure, yeah," I said. "I don't really mind what you do as long as it's safe and legal and makes you happy." Something troubled me. I was searching. "Wait a minute. What about the ring? What about the restaurants and limos—where did you get all your money, Blase?"

"Trust fund," he said, but he was talking to his fork. He let go of my hands, then he held up his napkin across his face, beneath his eyes, like a harem girl.

"A writer," I said. "Well, I guess you'll have to begin at the bottom."

"Actually," Blase said. "I've decided to start at the top and sit upon it."

After dinner, Blase and I got a cab and Blase directed the cabbie to the Plaza.

"But you told Jib we'd stop by," I said, not that I really wanted to see him. "He's expecting us."

"My darling Toby fiancée dear," he said. "It is always nice to be expected and not arrive," and he began kissing my neck.

That night, from our hotel room at the Plaza, I phoned my mother, father, sisters, and my best friend Claire to tell them the good news.

"You're gonna *marry* him?" Claire said.

"Yeah."

"Why?"

"You're supposed to say, 'I'm so happy for you!'"

"I'm so happy for you!" Claire said. "Are you pregnant?"

I phoned Carley and Alex, my two best friends from Andover, and Rosie Ripberger, my best friend from Harvard, knowing they'd hoot and holler and say the right things and they did.

Blase phoned his parents and then he phoned everyone else in New York, even people he didn't really know or like, including maître d's at some of the restaurants we frequented who congratulated him heartily though of course they had no idea who he was. We both spoke to David, thanked him for introducing us, asked him to be our best man, said things like, "If it weren't for you ... "

Blase ordered champagne and we toasted Us and he said, "Toby, you are the joy of my heart. I'll love you forever and I could never love you less," which had a funny ring to it, though I knew what he meant. Then we were glove and hand, almost one, and I know it sounds trite, but I couldn't imagine anyone in the world happier than me.

FIVE

It's the Bride and Groom!

Let the Muses sing! And the Graces dance!
Not at their wedding only, but all their days long.

Lying in bed in a royal blue room at the Plaza, listening to the buzz and hum of my fiancé asleep to my left, I was seized by the thought that I had just promised to spend the rest of my life with someone. Not just a little time—an afternoon, the weekend, the holidays, a season—but all of my time, the rest of my life. Whenever I spend long periods of time with someone, I make sure to bring my own transportation in case things begin to sour or get stale, in which case I can make a quick exit. But part of the idea of spending the rest of your life with someone is that there is no exit. You may build something solid and beautiful and safe together—or you may think you have only to discover, years later, that the house is on fire and the ladder's been kicked away.

I considered further drawbacks to spending the rest of your life with someone: your heart's desire will know your private nasty little quirks—that you pick your teeth with your pinkie nail, that you still enjoy the occasional Twinkie, that you bleach your otherwise dark lip hair, that you're not so pleasant to be around after a bowl of lentil soup. And you will learn things about him you never particularly wanted to know. And pretty soon, you will become ordinary to each other. After a while, even "my Jaguar" becomes "my car."

"Toby?"

"Hey, Mom. What's up?"

"Toby, it's four-thirty in the morning. What's wrong?"

"Sorry," I said. "I need to ask your opinion about something."

Silence.

"Mom?"

"Yes." Her voice was far away.

"Do you think someone can love something they'll have as long as they live? I mean, if you have something and you know that you'd have to die to lose it, can you really adore it? I mean, does anyone really love breathing?"

"Toby, is your asthma acting up?"

"I don't have asthma, Mom. You're thinking of Kate."

I heard another voice in the background, then Mom addressing the voice: "It's Toby. She's having an asthma attack."

"No, I'm not. I don't have asthma, Mom."

"So why did you say you're having trouble breathing?"

"I didn't," I said.

"So what's wrong?"

"Nothing. Who're you talking to?"

"Isabelle. Want to say hi?"

"Yeah."

A pause, then Isabelle's voice.

"Hey, Toby. I didn't know you had asthma."

"I don't."

"Oh. So why're you calling?"

"Tell me something, Iz. Do you honestly think someone can love another person for the rest of his life?"

"You're having second thoughts," Isabelle said.

"Not really."

"Toby, it's okay to have second thoughts. Really. It's perfectly natural. Maybe not this soon, not the very night of your engagement—" I heard Iz whisper, "She's having cold feet."

"I'm not having cold feet."

"You're not?" Some fussing with the phone, then Isabelle's whisper, "She's *not* having cold feet." Isabelle yawned into the receiver. "Sorry to be so dense, Toby, but is that why you're calling at four-thirty in the morning? To tell us you're not having cold feet?"

"I guess I just miss you guys."

"We miss you too, Toby. Here's Mom."

"I know you'll be very happy with Blase," Mom said. "Now get some rest. Good night, darling."

"Good night, Mom."

"Oh, don't forget: if things don't work out, you can keep the ring."

* * *

90

Replacing the receiver, I realized that it wasn't just the idea of being with *someone* for the rest of my life that was haunting me, it was the idea of being with someone I'd once judged to be pompous, chauvinistic and arrogant.

After two cigarettes and a soak in the tub, an excellent place to subdue and organize unruly mental items like vague Doubts, nameless Dread, and unspecified Guilt, I resolved that the name-dropping, coke-snorting, arm-waving, torso-lurching, loud-laughing, finger-snapping, sexist idiot whose acquaintance I made at David's was not *really* Blase. The *real* Blase was the romantic, kind, funny, generous, smart, and ambitious (if somewhat impetuous, hedonistic, clumsy, and fibbing) one I fell in love with, the one I'd been seeing these past five weeks, the one with the thick feet and the long head and the captivating gumball eyes who often said "I love thee," and the one I would marry.

Claire, my best friend, who was nothing if not frank and outspoken—the kind of person, I'm sorry to say, who would ask, "Who's the idiot?" right in front of the idiot, later excusing herself with, "I was just being honest," as if morality were plainly an excuse for immorality—Claire had told me she'd heard of Blase, he was best friends with Jib Foster, right? "I don't know him *personally*, Toby" she'd said, "but I know Jib's Trouble."

"So?" I'd said.

"So, Jib and Blase are best friends."

"So?"

"Figure it out, Toby."

"That doesn't make Blase Trouble. You're my best friend, Claire, and you're Trouble, but look at me."

"Right," she'd said.

People had told me, rather unhelpfully, to be on the lookout for nasty shocks and surprises on my wedding day. Things always happened, they said, things you hadn't prepared for, and all of a sudden you are called on to be graceful and resourceful, spur-of-the-moment. But no one dropped the wedding cake, the caterer showed, the photographer had film, and I didn't get my period. The nature of the disaster was, to my mind, totally unique, unheard of in modern wedding lore, and worse for the fact that its cause lay so close to my heart.

The night we became engaged, I'd phoned my mother and she'd said, "I s'pose you haven't set a date yet."

"Three weeks from Friday," I said.

"No."

"Yes."

"But, Toby, what about picking out patterns and registering at a department store and the engagement parties and the bridal showers and choosing your invitations and an ensemble and a chapel and a reception hall, and changing your mind about each of these three or four times—and, most importantly, having cold feet and crying and needing me to reassure you and finally realizing you're the happiest girl in the world?

Have you thought about all this, Toby? These things take *time*."

I explained to my mother that we wanted to be married in New York, to have an intimate wedding with close friends and family, a small reception—like a party—and I'd be making the invitations myself, sending them out next week.

Mom started crying. I was the first child to marry and here I was refusing to turn to her for advice and assistance, just when I needed her most. It broke her heart, she said. She'd always hoped I'd be married in Manchester, like she was, and her sisters and brothers were, and her mother and father were, and even some friend of hers she called her "best" but I'd never heard of. She couldn't believe I could be so selfish, except that she'd always known I was.

I talked it over with Blase and he finally agreed to be married in Manchester, once I convinced him Nathaniel Hawthorne was really from Manchester.

"Really?" Mom said. "Well, I did make some plans for that weekend, when it became clear you didn't want me around, but I s'pose I could cancel them."

I drew up a list of details to be attended to: flowers, food, location, apparel, transportation, etc. I was in charge of the guest list and invitations, Blase said he'd handle the music, and Mom said she'd do the rest—getting the nod from me first, on every detail, she promised. Saturday, I collected names and addresses from Blase, my mom, and Blase's mom—Blase and I decided we'd invite ten friends each, and our families could invite twenty-five each and that was it.

I struggled with the invitations for a while, mixing sunset scenes and loving profiles and Manhattan skylines and dreamy seascapes, finally settling on this:

Please come celebrate
the wedding
of

Toby Dodge
and
Blase Regenhere

12:00 noon, Saturday next
The Hearthside Inn
Manchester

Mom must have phoned twenty times that day.

"Do you want a rehearsal dinner?"

"No."

"A cocktail party the night before?"

"No."

"Do you want a ring bearer?"

"No."

"Do you want a flower girl?"

"No."

"Do you want to come down the aisle to 'Here Comes the Bride'?"

"No."

"Do you want a garter ceremony?"

"Definitely not."

"Do you want a band?"

"Blase is taking care of the music."

"Right. How 'bout a first dance with the father of the bride?"

"Me? No."

"A cake-cutting ceremony?"

"No."

"Tossing the bouquet?"

"Mother, no! I want a *party*. A simple, tasteful celebration. That's all."

"Well, it's *your* wedding, Toby. I wish you'd just keep it in mind that this day will set the tone for the rest of your life with Blase. If you want a humdrum marriage, so be it. I guess that's your choice."

Since I was a Ph.D. candidate and a Fellow, someone allegedly mature enough emotionally and intellectually to work at my own pace, I gave myself two weeks' vacation and Blase and I spent our last premarital days together in bed, eating black olives, bread, and cheeses, getting fizzy on wine and champagne, reading the real estate section, Yeats, and Keats out loud, and singing a song we made up called "We're Getting Married— Hi Ho! Hi Ho!" to the Looney Tunes tune and not only did we each lose five pounds, we also found a one-bedroom, two-story sublet in a brownstone in the East Sixties for $1000. Staying in bed for a week can be very productive.

During the drive up to Mom's, Blase and I discussed goodness, God, and truth until we reached Salem and Blase said it was time to get serious.

"Just tell me the taboos. With your mom, I know it's religion. What about your dad?"

"Turn here," I said, indicating the direction with my hand. "Money. Don't mention money. Having blown a fat trust and two monstrous inheritances, Dad's pretty sensitive about the issue. Aside from that, the usual: sex, drugs, politics."

"What about your sisters?"

"The sky's the limit. Turn this way at the stop," I said, pointing and nodding in the proper direction.

"Okay, I think I've got it: with your mom it's religion, your dad's money and the usual, and with your sisters it's the sky," Blase said.

"Right," I said. "Okay, turn that way here."

"Toby, there's one thing about you I need to know before I take you as my lawfully wedded wife," Blase said. "Why is it you never say 'right' or 'left'? You always point."

"I have a right-left distinction problem," I said.

"What! And just when were you planning to break this news of your handicap? After the wedding?" Blase was laughing. "It's extraordinary! You can't tell the difference? You must be murder at a square dance."

"I get the *words* confused," I said.

"Were you absent from kindergarten that day?"

"Blase!"

"Well, here's a trick I used: your right hand's the hand you pick your nose with."

"Ha, ha."

"So what is it—you can't distinguish right from left?"

"I can't reliably use the words, but my hands always get it right."

"Do you realize, Toby, that you would be utterly useless to a blind man who's lost his way? Has this ever occurred to you?"

I stared at my hands. I knew right from left, my *hands* knew it, but whenever I did venture to say the words, like when giving directions over the phone, it seemed I was guessing—and come to think of it, I always was.

"Good Christ—will you look at that?" Blase stopped the car.

"My God."

Blase was laughing. "Looks like Disneyland."

"That's *Mom's* house."

"I'm sure it's charming inside," Blase added.

The exterior of her house, a usually sober seventeenth-century colonial, was decorated like a child's birthday cake: about a hundred heart-shaped helium balloons were tied all along the gutters and even attached to the chimneys, crepe paper framed the doors and windows with huge silk flowers in the corners, and shoulder-high around the house was an enormous red ribbon, like Cartier's at Christmas, only it said, CONGRATULATIONS TOBY AND BLAZE!

"It doesn't usually look like this," I said.

By way of showing my indignation over the spectacle, I said, "Mom, 'Blase' is spelled with an *s*," but she was busy uncorking a bottle of champagne and ignored me.

She gave us glasses and raised hers and looked lovingly at Blase as she said, "To my future son! Oh, Blase!" and hugged him and kissed him and spilled champagne on him.

"You two will stay in the guest cottage, of course," Mom said. "I've had it cleaned and stocked with food and liquor and such."

I looked out the kitchen window and saw the guest cottage was also decorated for a kiddie party and its bow-sign said, "Love Nest." Grandma had been a proper, demure woman who never sported trousers or even panty hose and wore her fine snowy hair that had never known scissors or hair spray in a tidy Gibson Girl. Grandma's only sibling was a brother who did not believe in the existence of tasteful fashion trends or brown suits. So where did Mom come off being the sort of person who thought anything pink and frilly had to be worth the asking price? The sort of person who'd tear at soap operas, stick Santa on the roof at Christmas, paint her toenails red and wear light blue on her eyes, not to mention adding a Wurlitzer jukebox and a neon sign that flashed, GIRLS, GIRLS, GIRLS in our formal living room?

"Mom, we're staying at the Hearthside Inn tonight," I said.

"*What?*"

Luckily Blase said, "Holly, I decided it would be easier on Toby. If she stayed here, she'd undoubtedly be up with her sisters all night. This way, she'll be well rested for tomorrow." Mom smiled and said, "Of course." She adored Blase. Blase had all the virtues of an atheist and a stranger, and then some. He didn't seem constrained by thoughts of a watchful, fussy killjoy in the sky. He would be her son, her first, her only son. And best of all, he seemed to really like his liquor so she had a drinking partner, the one thing she'd really missed since Dad left.

Isabelle came running downstairs, kissed us hello, and grabbed me by the arm. "Come on," she said, and we hurried up to Anne's old room. Of course, Anne was prepping for a date and she looked beautiful, but Anne would look beautiful with the measles. My sisters started squawking at me, stroking my hair and checking out the ring and asking about my dress and the bouquet and babbling on about the wedding—I felt like somebody in a Jane Austen novel who had finally Made It—and I told them to knock it off. It would be simple and sweet, and the best part would be the charming little party afterward.

They shut up, gave each other significant looks. Then Iz gave me the bad news: "Uh, Toby, I guess you don't know that Mom rented the ballroom."

"The *ballroom*? For seventy people? That's absurd."

Then, the very bad news: "Well, they'll be a few more than seventy."

"What?"

"Mom invited a few people on her own."

I closed my eyes. "How many?"

Nobody said anything. "Go ahead," I said.

"A hundred."

"*What?*"

"Or so," Anne added helpfully.

Kate held my forearms. "Not to the wedding, though. She said you only wanted close friends at the wedding."

"I only wanted close friends period." Except for the *shish* of the brush in Anne's hair, it was dead quiet.

Then I said, "*Who?* Who are these hundred—*or so*—interlopers?"

Anne shrugged. "Mom's friends, I guess." Anne

was the one daughter who would never be in any peril of falling under the term "thinker."

"*Mom's friends*, you guess?"

"She said you wanted a party," Iz said. "And I s'pose her idea of a party is—"

"A hundred or so freeloading, glad-handing pifflers storming the open bar and thinking it's a wedding for Dottie and Case?"

My sisters were silent except for Anne, who wanted to know what a piffler was.

Blase and I were both angry, and though I was ready to put up a stink, I wasn't quite sure how to and Blase gently reminded me that stinks have their moments and clearly this wasn't one of them. So we said good night to my family and drove to the Hearthside Inn, where we got our next Happy Surprise: outside the inn, spelled out on a letter board, was: CONGRATU-LATIONS TOBY AND BLAZE. But that was nothing, really; it left us almost completely unruffled when we saw the message underneath:

HAVE YOUR WEDDING HERE!
ONLY $99
PER PERSON!

"There is only one thing to do at a moment like this, my dear," Blase said. He took my hand and hurried me into the hotel bar.

"Barkeep," Blase called, slapping his palm on the

bar. "Quick, sir—we need two of your most strengthening cocktails. Unless a double shot of vodka is administered posthaste, my wife will begin grand mal seizures—and it's not a pretty sight."

A grizzled-faced local sitting at the bar tapped Blase's shoulder. "That your *wife*? I thought it was your sister."

"Really? Actually, she's neither. She's my employee."

"Employee?" The man eyed me suspiciously. "What do you two do?" The man smoothed a hand over his T-shirted chest.

Blase put his arm around my shoulder. "I'm a magician and Glinda here is my Lovely Assistant."

"Magic, huh."

"Yeah, you know—disappearing acts, levitation, various stints with birds and rodents." Blase raised his glass and polished off his drink. "Darling, hurry up. I can see that seizure coming on." I smiled and downed mine.

"Barkeep? Quick, two more. And give our friend here another of what he's having."

The man's eyes passed from Blase to me and back to Blase. "You're at the Cabot in Beverly, aren't you?"

"The Cabot in Beverly?" Blase said. "Why, yes."

"Thought so. They always have that Grand David guy." The man's eyes narrowed. "You don't use dogs, do you?"

"What's that?" Blase said.

"Dogs. You don't use 'em in your act, do you?"

"Heavens, no. No dogs. Some fish, a dove or two,

rabbits, but never, under any circumstances, do we use dogs."

The bartender placed our drinks before us, said, "Here ya go, Stanley," and slid a sweaty mug toward the local. Stanley emptied his mug in one gulp. "You know what's funny about life?"

Blase and I waited until Blase realized Stanley was waiting for an answer. "What?" Blase said.

"You think you got somebody figured out and—bingo—she's gone. I mean, you give the woman everything—I don't mean you're *perfect*, no one's *perfect*, right? But you try real hard and you don't fool around, not once."

"So true," Blase said, nodding. "Barkeep? Another round." Blase turned to me. "I hate to be a nag, darling, but if you really want to get well, you're going to have to do better than this." He flicked a finger against the side of my glass. "You know what the doctor said."

After sliding another beer to Stanley, the bartender leaned toward Blase. "You're not driving, are you?"

"With Glinda in this delicate condition?" The bartender set our drinks on the bar.

Stanley swigged his beer. Then he cleared his throat and said, "So for seven years she's your woman. You count on each other, you know? You trust her. Then she takes it all and leaves with someone else. Seven *years*." Stanley was staring into his mug. He combed his hand into his hair and left it there. He looked like he might cry.

"Seven years," Blase said absently.

"Lucy and I had *dreams. Real* dreams." Stanley sighed and said, softly, "She took everything. She took my heart." He tilted his head way back and let the foam from his mug drain into his mouth. He tapped the empty mug on the bar. "She even took my dog."

"Well, that's awful," Blase said. "Just awful. Barkeep? Get my friend here another beer. He's earned it. Stanley, my friend, I know you'll work it all out. She'll come back to you and you'll go on and fulfill those dreams together. Or not, in which case you're better off without her." Blase turned to me. "Toby, it's time we bid farewell to our fine friend. We must rehearse."

" 'Bye," I said.

"Hey! I thought you said her name was Glinda," Stanley called after us.

We stumbled up to our suite, and Blase began singing a new version of last week's song: "We're Getting Married—We Should Have Eloped." But I thought about Stanley.

The wedding was at noon the next day. The room was small and bright with delicate white and gold wallpaper and six-foot trees full of sweetly fragrant white flowers. We walked up an aisle with thirty-five people per side, all our closest friends and family. I wore a white dress with a thousand tiny pleats pressed into the skirt but otherwise quite simple, and a crown of tiny white sweetheart roses. Blase wore a navy blue suit, a white rose pinned on a lapel, and everyone from my side thought he was an usher. We rehearsed with the reverend early that morning. "Like this?" I kept saying, making him watch my little bridal shuffle. "Or this?" taking carefully metered steps. "Fine. Sure. Anything. *Run* if you want. Just get up here," he said. Though he was officially jovial and gentle-mannered, and Claire called him the Marcus Welby of Ministers, privately he was a cranky old bastard who grilled us on the finer points of biology and parenting and made me feel like a sinner. But when we stood there before him, before God and our loved ones, I felt strong and pure and exhilarated. When I looked over at Blase he was smiling, but his knees were shaking and his face was shiny and a light shade of grey. The rev blabbed on about the sanctity of marriage and holy unions and, like a good Protestant, made a little gesture toward Jesus as if he were some old dead uncle who was footing the bill by way of his legacy, while we stood there mackerel-faced and motionless staring at him like he was a sergeant giving us orders, sneaking smiles at each other, until the script said, *Groom*: and then Blase, who got to go first, began to repeat The Words, loudly and clearly, at least till he got to "For richer for poorer," when his voice began to tremble. He was smiling, but tears were starting to spill out over his lids, his nose grew pink, and he rocked gently heel-to-toe and his voice grew softer and cracked like a teenager's, but with real determination he repeated, at a whisper: *To love and to cherish, till death do us part.* Then when it was my turn, I couldn't find a voice, any voice, Minnie Mouse's voice, though I did burp, then cry, really cry, I mean, except without all the noises since, for the most part, I held my breath until I thought I'd pass out and I suddenly had an image of Mom sprinting up the aisle, shoving everyone out of the way and saying, "*I'm* in charge."

When I began whispering my lines, I suddenly noted a kennel's worth of sniffling behind us and the rev raced through the rest of the ceremony and reported that we were husband and wife and our friends and family charged us, like football players after the guy with the ball, and hugged us and cried and, all in all, it couldn't have been a better first step into married life.

The reception was to start in an hour, so after lots of kissing and hugging, everybody skedaddled down to the bar (which Blase called "the swilling station") and I asked Mom to show us the ballroom.

"It's not going to be in the ballroom," she said.

"But Isabelle said—"

"Your sisters told me you were upset about that, so I had the party moved," and I mouthed, "Thank God" to Blase, who smiled and squeezed my hand as we followed her to an elevator that took us to the second floor.

"There are three rooms here," she said, "and I've had all the decorations moved."

The first room was the size of our den at home, appointed with five Windsor chairs with helium balloons tied to the back of each, a crazy web of crepe paper tacked to the ceiling, and ten or twelve flower arrangements on the floor. "This room will be for intimate conversations," Mom said. Then she led us down a hall to a second room, slightly larger, with seven or nine grey metal folding chairs also tagged with helium balloons, a mess of streamers on the ceiling, and flower arrangements on the floor. "This room," she said, "will be for people who are tired of all the music and loud noise—" "—and feel like relaxing on a cold metal chair," I said, and Mom, who was already well in her cups, smiled and said, "Right." She brought us to a short wide hall at the top of some stairs and opened a pair of dark double doors. "And this will be for the main part of the party." The room had a small dance floor, seven round tables covered with white cloths and enormous arrangements of flowers with helium balloons floating above them, a few ballooned metal chairs tucked in around the tables, and twisted streaks of crepe paper crisscrossing the ceiling, swirling down the walls like barber poles, half covering the old hunting prints on the mahogany panels—obviously this room was for small, casual, North Shore parties and get-togethers, like witchcraft trials and wakes. Like the other two rooms, this one had no windows.

I went back into the hall. A man and woman were setting up a bar in front of the railing at the top of the stairs and I froze. Between the slats of the railing you could see the ballroom, people hustling in, a band playing lively calypso music, the bride and groom twirling on the huge dance floor.

"There's *another* wedding?" I said.

"Oh, yes," Mom said. "And they were kind enough to trade this space for the ballroom at the last minute."

"Of course they were," I said. "This place is hideous!"

Mom pouted. "You don't like it?"

"It'd be perfect for a funeral—" I said.

"She loves it," Blase said, and took my mother's arm. "You know Toby's just a little thrown off by last-minute changes."

"Right," Mom said, all smiles again.

"How did you manage to uninvite people?" I said.

"Oh, I didn't uninvite anyone."

"Mom, we're not going to be able to fit two hundred people up here!"

"Sure we will—there's plenty of space," Mom said. "Besides, weddings are supposed to be intimate."

"What about the band, Blase? Where're we going to put the band?"

"Darling, we couldn't fit a band up here, so I gave the Robertses the band and they gave us their deejay," Blase said.

"*The Robertses?*"

"The people down there," Blase said. "They were awfully decent about it, too."

"You *knew* about this?" It was a conspiracy.

"Holly told me just before the wedding started, and I didn't tell you then because I didn't want to upset you," Blase said.

"But I might have been able to *do* something about this then," I said and stomped a foot, for the first time understanding why a child stomps her feet: What else can you do when everything's out of your control and nothing's going your way?

"Holly," Blase said, "I'm going to take Toby

107

upstairs for a minute to freshen up and cool down."

"Right," Mom said and she hurried across the hall to talk with the Robertses' caterer, who was fussing with meatballs in a dish on one of those metal pretzel carts.

"Damn! What about *dinner*?" I called. "What're we gonna do—order out for pizzas and eat on the floor?"

"Just hors d'oeuvres, Toby," Mom said. "We'll be serving lots of lovely hors d'oeuvres." When she saw my face she added brightly, "We're saving a fortune, honey," as if saving money were the point of a wedding reception.

Upstairs, Blase opened a bottle of champagne and then made sense of everything for me.

"Look," he began, "it may not be exactly what you wanted, but our friends'll still be here, there'll still be dancing and celebrating, and, sweetheart, you are my wife."

I felt better but sulked a little more and guzzled my champagne.

"You'd better fix your makeup," Blase said. "Your mascara's made a beeline for your nose."

After I splashed cold water on my face, fixed my makeup, brushed my hair, adjusted my crown of roses, and had two more glasses of champagne, I was smiling. Blase was my husband. I was his wife. The purpose of the day had been fulfilled and nothing, I thought, could really touch the beauty and sanctity of that.

Blase sat me down on the bed and handed me a black velvet box.

"When my grandfather married my grandmother, he gave her this. When my father married my mother, he gave her this. And now, I am giving this to you, Toby, because you are my wife, and I love you with all my heart, and with every cell that has a claim to being mine."

It was an open filigreed bracelet with a diamond clasp.

"It's lovely," I said.

"It's platinum," Blase said. Then we took off all our clothes.

We could hear the commotion before the elevator even stopped on two. The doors opened to a crowd of people smushed together, and the man and woman who rode down with us smiled and exchanged glances and the woman said, "What's going on here?"

"A wedding," I said, smiling and kissing Blase.

"You one of the bridesmaids?" the man asked, and I snubbed him and almost stepped on the train of a long red dress belonging to a very bleached blond with black goo smeared around her eyes like glasses. Her dress must have been sewn on her, the extra fabric trailing behind about six feet. I smiled at her. She didn't return the smile, but she stuck her tongue in the hole at the bottom of her plastic champagne cup. *At least she's not from our side,* I thought. When all is going badly, I've found, it's the little things that comfort.

Blase and I squished our way into the wide hall. Lots of people. Lots of strange people elbow-to-elbow. Men dressed in lime jackets and polyester plaid jackets and no jackets, just sport shirts. Women with potatoey bodies in bright clingy dresses and teased-up hair, with loud shrill laughs, teetering on shiny heels, drinking bourbon and gin. I found myself feeling better and better when I realized Blase's family had such tacky friends. I held tightly to Blase's arm and we waited at the top of the stairs to greet our guests, none of whom arrived for the five minutes we stood there, so we pardoned our way to the bar and ordered a couple of vodka tonics.

"If it isn't the groom agog, breathlessly anticipating the first fornical night with the blushing bride . . . " Jib had slung his arm around Blase's shoulders and was talking to Blase's ear. "Tranquing the baser passions, I see, hoping to survive all the glad-handing and air-kissing with Uncle Impotent and Aunt Bulimia." Blase turned and Jib gave him a hug, they slapped backs and laughed. Then Jib noticed that I happened to be there and quickly leaned his cheek toward mine, not touching it or anything, and he made a little smack near my ear. Leaning back, tilting his head right, then left, Jib said, "Hey, whose is that?"

"Whose is what?" I said.

"The dress," he said. "Whose is it?"

"*Mine,*" I said. Jib and Blase looked at each other and laughed.

"I mean who *makes* it," Jib said.

"I don't know," I said, and Blase pulled back the fabric at the nape and said, "Signature Collections, of course," and he and Jib laughed again and Jib said, "Of *course*. They really *are* unsurpassed in bridal couture." I downed my vodka tonic.

"Hey, who are all these monsters, anyway?" Jib said, apparently referring to our guests, and I turned back to the bar and ordered another vodka tonic.

Funny thing: I was scared of Jib, mainly of his caustic manner and appearance and the feeling that he might really be able to see all the insecurities huddled together, quivering in my heart, and bring them out into bright light for examination, holding them up one by one and laughing—but I was also scared of the power he seemed to have over Blase.

Jib's face was as wide as Edward G. Robinson's at the cheeks and it called to mind vanilla pudding, though it looked firmer, as though you'd leave a belly button or a dimple if you pressed it, or stretch out across the room all stringy like silly putty or well-chewed gum if you pinched and pulled it. And Jib had rosy blubbery lips that he bit and sneered and pouted with a lot, eyes like almonds resting on the pointy end, somewhat startled eyes but they gave him a vicious startled look, not a sweet startled look like Blase's. Jib was surprisingly tall but sort of soft looking all over like he was covered with a layer of frosting. If Jib had been a gangster, they would have called him "Bubba." All in all, he called to mind a bad-ass Pillsbury Dough Boy with a few years on him, so it was odd that everyone seemed to consider him good-looking. And all that incredible charm and wit and brilliance that wowed Blase, that he thought Jib possessed by the truckload, were completely lost on me.

While Blase and Jib muttered and hee-hawed I polished off another vodka tonic and tried to ignore the red-nosed man in loud plaid to my left who suddenly seemed to be coming on to me until I told him I sold insurance, which Blase had told me is almost guaranteed to get horny old blisters, bad-breaths, and other unwanteds to pack up their old jokes and one-liners and move on.

Suddenly, arms around me, hair in my eyes, wet kisses on my cheeks.

"Toby! Jesus, you look like a *virgin*!" Carley said.

"No, she looks like a *princess*," Alex said.

"Same thing."

My two best friends from prep school, the women who were once girls I'd pulled all-nighters and panty raids with, broken curfew and parietal hours with, survived standardized testing, first loves, and personal crises with. Now we were grown-up and I was getting married and they were here at my wedding, just as we'd envisioned twelve years ago.

"Where's the mister?" Carley said.

I turned, gestured toward Blase. "That's him."

"Cute!" Alex said, but Carley just smiled. While Alex had always had an uncanny ability to say the right thing, the gracious thing, the thing I wanted to hear and would have scripted myself had my life been a play, it was Carley who could really comfort or console, whose opinion I valued, since her words were always expressions of her feelings and her feelings were always appropriately aligned with the truth. She said what she meant and was exactly who she was.

Blase put a hand on my shoulder.

"May I have the pleasure of an introduction to these ravishing Sabine maidens?"

Carley rolled her eyes and Alex giggled.

Blase said he'd heard so much about Carley and Alex, it was great to finally meet them, and how did we all know each other again?

Jib appeared behind Blase and said something to his ear as people pushed their way to and from the bar, clutching glasses, arms raised above the crowd, moving tentatively, like children wading in a pool of frigid water.

Squeezing my hand, Carley said, "We're gonna go say hi to your mom." She leaned to my face and said, softly, "Be happy." Then more kisses and Carley and Alex stepped into the crowd and were swept off toward the main room.

Blase slipped his arm around my waist. "Jib says he has some killer blow."

What was he talking about? Those days were over. We were Mr. and Mrs. Grown-up now. As I was searching for something to say, Anne approached, looking like one of those little fairies from the thirties in a pale pink dress with folds of sheer pink fabric flowing from the shoulders. She was beautiful, Anne was, I mean really delicate and tiny with a heart-shaped face and long strawberry curls.

"Care to dance?" she said to Jib.

"Think I'll give it a miss," Jib said. "Catch me later."

"May I have this dance?" Blase said, and offered her his arm.

"Can I get you a drink?" I said to Jib.

"You'll never remember what it's called," he said and went to the bar to get it himself. Then things really began to get stiff.

"So, where'd you go to school?" Jib asked. I couldn't believe such questions still seemed relevant to him.

"Harvard and NYU now."

"Uh-*huh*," he said. "You majored in English, right."

"Philosophy."

"I was an English major, too."

"Where'd you go to school?" I was trying, I told myself. This was trying. An attempt to make friends with Blase's best friend.

Jib looked at me goggle-eyed, as if Everyone knew he'd gone to Hampshire. "I'm writing a book now," he added.

Silence.

"Think about it," Jib said. "Right now, all over this dinky city, children are being molested, beaten, women are being raped, men are being knifed, their tongues cut out and eaten by primitive inbred psychopaths. It's something, isn't it?"

It's my wedding day, I thought, *and I don't want to think about the horror show of the world outside and you're a sick sonofabitch* and I said, "Yeah, it's something," and Jib began to laugh.

"People's lives being ruined, utterly destroyed, in a moment's bad luck," he said. He was still laughing. "Even here, odds are we have assorted felons: a few rapists, child abusers, embezzlers, probably a murderer or two. Definitely some drug addicts." He laughed, sniffled, took a sip of his drink. Then his eyes bugged. "Hey, look at that idiot in the Ralph Lauren jacket—purple and red?"

Suddenly Blase, dragging a few feet of crepe paper, and Anne, looking a bit peeved, elbowed their way back over to us. "Low ceiling," Blase said, pulling off the streamers, and Anne said, "Mom says Blase has to dance with you first."

"Kindly tell Mom that I'm pretty sure that it's my wedding and I've said it's okay."

Jib looked Anne up and down and said, "What's your name again?" and Anne said, "Anne."

Blase, basically a fun-lover who hadn't noticed the plummeting of the local fun factor, looked at Jib's drink. "What're you having, buddy?"

"Stoli," he said.

"Can I have a sip?" Anne said, and Jib looked at her and it seemed he suddenly noticed she was beautiful and said, "Why, of course you can, sweetheart," and held the glass to her lips.

"Yum!" she said, and Jib smiled and said, "My dear, there was a great deal of truth in what you just said, and you looked very pretty while you said it, which is much more important." Then he offered to get her her own and Anne said, "Gee, thanks!" and I shook my head and again found myself skeptical about Mom and Dad's claim that Anne was their natural child, and the oldest. She had a bite-sized vocabulary and her expletives included "icky," "yucky," "neat-o," "wow," "keen," and "super." But she was beautiful and sweet and lots of men still seem to be charmed by stupidity in the female.

Jib patted Blase's shoulder, and looking past me, into the crowd, said, "So anyone here? Hmmm. *Red.*" I turned and spotted the very bleached blond putting both hands in her hair and smiling at Jib, who said, "Nature calls," and slid off.

Blase put his arm around me. "I guess we'd better go in," he said, gesturing toward the biggest room, the room with the dance floor, the room where our parents were milling around with lots more people we didn't know.

Taking my hand and smiling, like we were walking down the aisle again, Blase said, "Excuse us, excuse us," to clumps of people, some of whom had bits of streamers on their shoulders and in their hair, who gave us annoyed looks like we were so rude, and we made our way into the room and all of a sudden, as Blase was excusing us across the dance floor toward our parents, to safety, we heard, loud and scratchy, like an announcement at a baseball game, *"And here come the bride and groom!"* and all these people began to look around, turning their heads, going, "Where?" "Where?" "Is *that* them?" and Blase whispered, "Smile so they'll know it's us," and I smiled and just then the deejay began to play "To All the Girls I've Loved Before," and we kept pushing and shoving our way through the knot of people as the deejay repeated, *"Yes, it's the bride and groom!"* as if we were some sort of shiny new fuel-injected prize on a game show, and it seemed our parents were miles away ("To all the girls I once caressed . . . ") and like we'd never make it across that dance floor to them ("I'm glad you came along . . . ") so when I reached my mom I hugged her like a buoy in the middle of a storm, which she mistook as a sign of gratitude and elation, and said, "You're loving it, aren't you?"

"Who *are* all these people?"

"Old friends of ours," Mom said. "People who've known and loved you for years." And then I recognized some of them: it was the grocer staring down that woman's dress; rolling onions up the side of his martini glass, tossing them in the air with his tongue, then catching them in his open mouth was the pool man, Joe; and the three men chugging beers by the bar and slapping each other hard on the back were the gas station owner and two of his pumpers, one of whom was a short, frizzy-haired, round-assed kid who used to wink at me in my teens and call me "hot pants." Then I saw three of our old housekeepers, the balding old woman from down the street, a gardener my dad had to fire because he started growing pot in the greenhouse—it was a domestic nightmare from my childhood.

When I spotted the very bleached blond dipped in red with the raccoon eyes I whispered to Mom, "At least *she's* not from our side," and Mom said, "Oh that's Annie Titus's little girl—remember Lisa? Isn't she all grown up now?"

"I gotta go," I said to Blase, and dashed out of the room, my rose crown knocked off by the low streamers, the deejay behind me noting, *"And there goes the bride!"* Where were my sisters? Where were my friends?

Iz grabbed me at the elevator.

"You okay?" she said. Her eyes were glazed and she was weaving a little.

"Do you recognize these people?"

"Yeah," she said. "What a *goof!* Mom even invited Mr. Nealy!" Mr. Nealy was the man in charge of garbage collection in Salem and groundskeeper of the cemetery. Then she noticed I was a bit disgruntled, if not to say wild, by the way I was grinding my teeth and punching a fist into a palm, and said, "Toby, you can't ask them to leave, so you might as well try to enjoy yourself."

"How'm I gonna do that?"

"Get drunk."

I got drunk. Blase got drunk. Our families got drunk. The blue-collars and former domestics got drunk. The rest of our friends finally arrived. They'd gotten drunk in the bar downstairs and spent an hour in the ballroom getting more drunk before they realized it wasn't our wedding reception. At last my dad materialized and he was drunk. "Where were you?" I said.

"Getting drunk downstairs. I thought—"

"Yeah, yeah," I said.

Suddenly the deejay's voice came booming from the room: "*Where* are *the bride and groom?*"

Blase and I bolted for the elevator, but my mother grabbed my arm. "There you are, you two," she said, and led us into the room, to two metal helium-ballooned seats that had been placed in the middle of the floor like electric chairs for a public execution.

"Oh, God," I said.

"*Everybody clear out!*" the deejay said. "*Make space for the bride and groom!*" and people did clear out, edging off to the side of the dance floor, stepping on each other's feet, elbowing and head-bumping and looking very cross, leaving us vulnerable, terrified, in those two chairs.

"*And* now," the deejay began, "*a special treat from an anonymous donor!*"

Whatever humiliation we were about to endure, I knew it would be on account of my mother. And right then, sitting in that chair, next to my new husband, with all the eyes of all these drunks, my new family, strangers, semistrangers, and close friends stuck on me, I realized that this so-called party wasn't about Blase and me at all: it was about my mother. And I realized that my whole life, all our parties—birthday parties, sledding parties, horseback riding parties, even holiday parties—were populated with drunken adults milling around and telling us to get lost or go get them another drink and *they were all about my mother*, and I wanted to scream "Damn you!" but we were stuck there, trapped now, set up—for her amusement.

And then it happened. Someone entered the room wrapped head to toe in a black blanket, face hidden deep in the folds of a hood, and set a little tape player on the floor, pushing a button with a bony white finger; very small metallic music, the kind hookah-toking hippies always had in the background, the kind that bore a vague resemblance to snake-charming music, began to trickle and squeak into the room. Then, as if revealing a work of fine art rendered in Carrera marble with the wisest Italian hands, the person let the blanket drop, slowly, and raised both arms, like a gymnast punctuating a perfect execution, and the room was silent, except for that twangy, scratchy music, because standing before us, facing Blase and me, as if she had some connection with us, represented or belonged to us, which for a very long moment I guess she did, was a middle-aged woman dressed like I Dream of Jeannie, heavily painted and powdered and bearing the words CONGRADULATIONS TOBY & BLAZE grease-penciled across her stomach, above the glittering rhinestone in her belly button, which words began to quiver and shrink and stretch with the orbiting of her hips. Arms raised, twirling around us with braceleted arms and bejeweled feet, the woman smiled at us and Blase leaned over to me and said, "I'm stopping this."

And God, I was with him on that, really I was, but I knew if he jumped up, said, "Enough, harem girl! Be gone!" or if, what was more likely, we just rose from our little chairs and skulked out of the room, then the reception would seem to be even more of a disaster than it already was, and our friends would be horrified and talking about the catastrophe for years. I stared at the crowd, now silent, frozen, and gaping at us, at the woman. Carley, Alex, Claire, David, Della, and Rosie, my college friend who'd taught me to take myself seriously, who'd made it here all the way from Seattle. I wanted to cry but I fixed a fake smile on my face, one that I hoped said, "Isn't this silly, light-hearted amusement?" One thing I've learned from the advertising world is that if you claim something's funny or tasty or gets rid of wrinkles, and if you back this up with a performance that's a shoo-in for the Oscars, then people buy it even if the thing is basically water and dirt. Blase credited the theory especially when I assured him that his role of sultan would end

soon, it *had* to end soon, or at least it had to *end*, and
when it did, we could crawl off and renew our buzzes
with some more brain tinglers and fizzies upstairs. So
we sat there like two slabs of cheddar, fake-smiling,
fake-wowing, fake-hand-clapping, and rocking-back-
and-forth. Fake-loving it. When the woman wrapped
a turquoise sash around Blase's neck—oh, ho, ho!—
and pulled Blase to his feet—ha, ha!—he looked at me
in despair, like a puppy on his way to the gas chamber,
but he moved with her, shaking his hips back and
forth—oh, là, là!—and I faked-finding this oh-so-
very-amusing, and everyone, checking our reactions,
began to laugh and find it oh-so-very-amusing and I
was secretly planning ways to murder my mother. My
only consolation, I thought, was that my mother had
the presence or absence of mind to announce this
"gift" as from an unidentified person.

Finally the woman let Blase sit down and handed him a bottle of champagne—"Oh, thank you!
We've never tried Bernie's Bubbles"—gave each of
us a kiss—awhh—and left. It was over. It was over.
And people were clapping. As we rushed from the
room, we heard people starting to whisper, "Who
did it?" "Was it *Jib*?" and I turned around and
wished I'd had a gun because there was my mother,
waving at everybody, fake-covering her face with
her hand and shrugging her shoulders like, "Wasn't
I naughty?" and actually rising from her chair and
taking bows.

Blase and I ran for the elevator, stepping on people's feet, shoving them out of the way, and suddenly
there was my mother beside me, smiling and giggling.

"You're not *mad*, are you?" she said, fake-sheepishly.

"*I could kill you,*" I actually said, and she found this an amusing little joke.

"You *loved* it," she said, "I could tell. And besides, photos don't lie," and she held up five Polaroids of Blase and me loving-it, and she kissed my cheek, and disappeared toward the bar.

Humiliation is an enormously difficult thing to endure: doing so makes you a cheese; not doing so makes you rude or selfish. Of course, if the only members of the audience are the members of your family, then you're always entitled to be rude or selfish. But add friends, your new in-laws, their friends, domestics, your pool man, and a whole lot of strangers, and put your mother behind it, and you discover the dual nature of your identity: you find yourself almost automatically cheesing, and at the same time you realize that, contrary to everything you've believed about yourself your entire life, you are quite capable of brutal, cold-blooded murder.

Standing by the elevator, looking at our feet, hoping no one would identify us, in spite of our having been pointed out all afternoon by that deejay (who, I should have known, was equal to my mother in terms of bad taste, a willing accomplice, since he wore white tassel loafers and a seventies mustache, and called me "Babe" and Blase "Stud"), someone tapped my shoulder and I pretended I didn't feel it. Tap. I tried to act like,

Don't bother. I'm not who you think I am; you've mistaken me for someone else, a tough way to act without saying or doing anything.

"Toby!" It was Claire and David. Claire hugged me and stroked the back of my head.

"I love the flowers," she said.

"It's a fiasco."

"I met David" she said, putting her arm around him. "He's a doll."

David grinned and shucks-ed. Then he embraced me.

"I want to murder my mother."

"I'm not sure that many people really saw, what with all those balloons and things." Claire was forcing a smile.

"I liked the balloons," David said.

"Claire, everybody saw. I saw them see. And no one will forget. From time to time they'll tell the story about how someone's mother hired a stripteaser for her wedding. And while Blase and I are headed back to New York, phone lines will be buzzing all over the country: 'Guess what? You won't believe what the mother of the bride did . . . ' And years from now, we'll be living in Dubuque and I'll be in the supermarket and some old lady will say, 'Aren't you Mrs. Regen-here?' and clasp her hands over her head and shimmy and laugh."

"Not Dubuque," Blase said.

David smiled. "But it's so typical of your mother, Toby. Really, I was amazed when you said you guys were coming back here to get married." David and I grew up together, he'd known my mother about as long as I had. "You're lucky it wasn't worse."

"*Worse?* How could it have been *worse?*"

"*She* could have danced."

"Well, it's over," Claire said. "And the wedding itself was beautiful and I'm very happy for you guys."

"Thanks," I said, and we all kissed.

"Aren't you going to say good-bye to everybody?" Claire said.

"What are we s'posed to say? 'So long. Sorry we have to miss the geeks and contortionists . . . ' Won't you do it for us? Tell them we were late for our plane or something?"

"Sure thing."

When I started crying on the plane, Blase said, "I hope you're crying because you're almost half as happy as I am, Toby," and gave me a long kiss. Actually, I was thinking about my mother, about a bedtime story she told us when we were kids.

A little girl goes shopping one day with her mother. It is during a black and grey time called the Depression when everyone's poor and eating garbage. The mother has to get some elastic bands or envelopes. At the front of the store, the little girl sees something so beautiful she lets her mother walk on and she just stands and stares. It is a doll, a doll as big as the girl, with noodle-curls to her shoulders, a pink dress with frills and ribbons, and shiny black party shoes. A man comes up to the little girl and says, "You like that doll, don't you, honey?" and the little girl tells him it's the most beautiful thing she's ever seen.

"Why don't you ask your mommy to buy it, then?"

"We're very poor," the little girl says. The man smiles at the little girl, takes the doll from the shelf, and hands it to her. "This is my store," he says, "and now this is your doll."

When the little girl shows the doll to her mother, her mother does not say anything. Her mother does not smile, but takes the little girl's hand and they leave the store, ride the bus back to Salem, where they live in a room off an alley behind a Chinese restaurant. The mother finds a big box and puts all the little girl's toys in it, except for the doll. "I'll bring this to the Salvation Army when I leave for work," she says. The mother has to work late into the night. There is no dad.

In the bigger world, war is going on; the city has blackouts and all the lights must be turned off. The mother tells the little girl to hide under the kitchen table if there is a blackout, not to move. That night, the siren sounds and the little girl turns off the lights, and takes the doll with her under the table. The doll is hard and her fingers are pointed. The little girl holds the doll tight, and waits for the mother to get home. She closes her eyes and counts to a hundred then back to zero, spells her name and the names of all the kids in her class, and waits and shakes because she has to go to the bathroom but she cannot move from under the table. She puts the doll's hand in her mouth, but it is hard and sharp, not a soft little bite like her Baby

Dee's had been. She waits to the sounds of dirty men in the alley, laughing, breaking glass, urinating, tapping on the window, jiggling the doorknob.

By the time the mother comes home, the little girl is asleep with her doll under the table. They are lying in a pool of cold liquid. The doll must be thrown away.

"Do you know who that little girl was?" my mother said.

"Who?" we asked.

"That little girl was me," she said, and she started to cry and ran out of the room.

Did this explain anything about why my mother had ruined my wedding? Probably not, but the whole flight back to New York, I couldn't get it out of my head. It made me think, and that's for sure.

Six

The Salad Days

It's often said that you never really know someone till you've walked around in his shoes. But why should walking around in someone else's *shoes* yield the desired knowledge of the *other*? After all, it's still *you*, with all of your desires and beliefs and prejudices and past experiences and expectations, doing the walking—and chances are, if the person's shaped anything like Blase, the shoes don't fit anyway. What I wanted, what I thought I had, with Blase was knowing what he, *that guy*, the one with the big head and the skinny chest and the gum ball eyes and the squirrelly laugh, was like in his heart of hearts.

But put the man in the company of construction workers and he'll drink beer from cans, wolf-whistle, scratch his balls, and burp. Invite him to a nuclear arms debate and watch him holler "Disarmament Now!" with the cons, speak the sober, starchy language of Cold War and deterrence with the pros, and remain absolutely blank-faced and silent otherwise. Among outdoorsmen, he's the burly hunter, camper, angler: "I've always loved fly-fishing!" he once exclaimed when David told us he was planning a week on the Test. "But you've never fly-fished," I said. Blase, not one to let it stand that he'd been caught in a lie, scratched his big head, then offered, "I mean, I've always liked *the idea* of fly-fishing." Blase was dandy with the dandies, snotty with the snots. With women, he was pro-choice, for affirmative action and the ERA; with Jib, he talked about bimbettes, squeezes, and babes; with me, he sang the praises of commitment and fidelity. The more I learned about Blase, the more tenuous became my grip on who he really was.

Shortly after the wedding, Blase told me his trust fund had run out; we'd have to live on my stipend. Was that okay?

"I'll have to start teaching," I said, "which will take a lot of time away from my thesis, which sounds great to me."

By this time, I was beginning to suspect my chosen field wasn't exactly what the ads had promised.

My philosophical career had begun rather modestly at the age of eleven when I happened upon a book in my father's library somewhat superciliously titled *Philosophy*, containing lofty, noble words like Virtue, Wisdom, and Truth. For a good half hour I struggled over the text until I had satisfied myself that I knew more than when I'd started, having made the sudden discovery that the subject at hand was *causal*, and not *casual*, relations.

When I decided to go to graduate school in philosophy, to commit myself to wisdom and truth for once and for ever, I was drunk on the ancients, saw myself eventually ascending from the everyday world of shadow and illusion into the full light of Platonic heaven, someday reaching a profound understanding of the world as it is in itself. Like most, I had entered graduate school with a wide-eyed optimism that came from graduating at the top of my class, with honors and awards and my choice of graduate schools, and from a total misunderstanding both of the difficulty of the subject and of the current philosophical climate. I saw myself mining the metaphysical terrain and digging up deep, recondite truths somehow overlooked by earlier excavators like Aristotle and Hume. I saw myself suddenly grasping not simply the truth about personal identity, my chosen area, but about the entire universe—like Newton, I would have a wholly original vision; like Einstein, I would draw the big picture and it would be shocking; and like Aristotle, Leibniz, Spinoza, Descartes, Locke, Berkeley, and Hume, I would write it all down in a treatise, something unheard of in twentieth-century philosophy, and everyone would thank me.

More than this, I would be joining the ranks of the most rational, the people who thought deeply about the most difficult questions, people who were dedicated to sorting things out, who lived by the Aristotelian credo "Distinguo!", who brandished Ockham's razor and with it sliced through nonsense directly into the heart of things. Philosophers must be wiser, kinder, more principled than other human beings, I thought. Their actions must be justified by higher moral laws. Their thoughts must flow and dovetail, one into another, in an orderly, precise fashion. Their lives, above those of all others, must make sense. The idea of entering the ranks of those governed by Reason, for whom Truth is queen and Order is second nature, spoke to something that burned in me, that sent me running from my little dorm room as an undergraduate and into an empty night, looking up toward an infinite and indifferent universe and issuing a long, steady cry for objective standards, for rational order, for meaning.

To arrive at NYU and learn that our philosopher of science was cheating on his wife, sleeping with the contemporary ethics professor's wife, while the contemporary ethics professor was addicted to gambling and triple-X porn, and to overhear our swashbuckling young philosopher of religion tell our chairman, a kindly old logician, that he didn't really think blacks and women could do philosophy, they didn't have "the stuff," he said, was to realize I'd been had. I felt like a disciple of Sun Myung Moon who, after pledging his life and soul to the reverend, suddenly realizes that the holy one can't fly or even float, except metaphorically which isn't flying or floating at all, that he is earthbound and mortal, limited by the same laws as everyone else. My consolation, then, had to come from my work. Truth could still be mine; I could still be wise.

So you might say it was something of a letdown to find myself in my fourth year of study, tinkering with demonstratives and indexicals, trying to construct coherent counterexamples to minor entailments of possible corollaries of someone or other's theory of reference, and picking apart definitions of terms. When I had thought I would be inquiring about the essence of a person, about what makes that person uniquely *that person*, I was told to examine the sentence "S is p." When I had undertaken an investigation of knowledge, I was told to examine the sentence "S knows that p." And when I had decided to delve into the nature of meaning, I was told to work out the entailments of the sentence "S means p by 'q'." What I had assumed would be lush terrain was really a desert landscape where there's only one guy, S, who apparently is or means or knows only one thing, p.

By my third year, I'd slid from my previous unjustified optimism beyond humility and into total despair. Every time I'd arrive at what seemed a plausible philosophical position and begin to work at its proof, I'd hear Wittgenstein, always Wittgenstein, "But is *that* how we use the word?" And if I'd start to think about it, to scribble out a few deductions, he'd shout, "Don't think, but *look*!" When I'd climb in bed at the end of the day, turn out the light and try to ease into a pool of nothingness, his voice would rise to the surface of my consciousness, and like a bubble the words would burst in my ears:

> *The results of philosophy are the uncovering of one or another piece of plain nonsense and of bumps that the understanding has got by running its head up against the limits of language.*
>
> *Philosophy is nothing but a house of cards.*
>
> *Philosophy only states what everybody admits.*
>
> *Philosophy leaves everything as it is.*

The man was ubiquitous, and his shadow obscured all my work, reduced my self-conception as a lone pioneer in the metaphysical firmament to that of a picky grammarian fussing over definitions of words everyone already understands anyway.

So teaching would justify my slacking off on my work.

Soon after we moved into our apartment, people began phoning for Blase late at night, people who didn't offer me greetings, people whose voices I didn't recognize. I'd stand facing Blase, mouthing, "Who is it?" while he shrugged his shoulders, then laughed and nodded and said, "Sorry, bro. No can do." Other times we might be in bed reading when our buzzer would sound and Blase would scramble downstairs to answer it. I'd hear voices, Blase's laugh, a snap, then Blase would return to the bedroom, shaking his head.

When I'd ask who it was, Blase would say a friend, an old colleague from Columbia, a former student.

"What'd they want?"

A phone number, an address, a reference.

"At this time of night?"

"I know. Can you believe it?"

I pushed him on it, but he didn't budge until the night I answered the phone, asked, "Who's calling?" instead of handing it immediately to Blase.

Blase said, "Is it for me?"

"Jimmy?" I said. "Oh, Blase told me to take a message."

Blase reached for the receiver but I turned away.

"It's okay. I'm his wife."

Blase was whispering, "Toby. Give it here," but I ignored him and stood on a chair when he went for the receiver again.

"Uh-huh. Sure. Fine," I said and hung up. "Jimmy wants two grams. He'll be over in twenty minutes."

"Shit!" Blase threw on a robe, scrambled downstairs, and waited for the buzzer. From the top of the stairs I heard a man's voice but I couldn't make out the words. Then Blase: "Not me. Not no more. Hey, sorry. Really. Try the Dinky. You know Tumbleweed, right?"

"Isn't there something you want to tell me?" I said when he'd dismissed Jimmy and climbed back in bed.

"Like what?"

"Like what the hell's going on. Who the hell Jimmy is. Why these strangers call so late, come to the house. Like—"

"Toby," he said, stretching it out, as if giving himself a moment to think.

"Yeah?"

After a long moment Blase said, "Truth is, I never really had a trust fund."

I laughed. "What does that have to do with anything?"

Blase was looking at his fingernails.

"And what do you mean you never had a trust fund?" I said. He couldn't *mean* that he never had a trust fund. All during our courtship, it was clear the man was loaded to the teeth.

Blase picked at a cuticle. "I mean I never had a trust fund."

"Then what'd you do? *Steal* all that money you were throwing around?"

"I was dealing."

"Dealing drugs?" No, cars. God, he made me feel naive sometimes.

"Coke."

I remembered sitting with Blase by the river: "My father's dead," he'd said.

"Do you hate me?" he said. He waited.

I scratched at my scalp.

"I needed the money. After I got canned, I needed the money. You just can't hang around certain people and places in New York without money—and I knew I'd never even meet a girl like you if I was broke. The fact that I've stopped dealing shows how good you are for me, how much you've helped me get my life together again. Bunny, you've given me a clean slate."

A tabula rasa, I thought, *for a cocaine dealer. A drug dealer. No—an* ex-*drug dealer. Now that's behind him. He's changed. He's changed because of me. I am good for him.*

Then he added, "In part, I did it for you, Toby. I knew you needed to be treated like a queen, and it would take money to do that."

"Then why are all these people phoning you *now* looking for drugs?"

"Takes a while for word to get around, you know?"

I didn't say anything.

"It all began in junior high," Blase said.

"What!"

"Mondays I got my allowance and I'd go down

134

to the store and clean out the candy counter. Next day, I'd bring it to school in a shoe box and sell it. There was an incredible demand and I was the only source so I made a killing." Now he was laughing, rocking back and forth, *snap*—forget about the coke: this was the *real* story and wasn't it a riot?

I asked was there anything else I should know. Were there children somewhere in the world with his last name who called him Daddy? Was he a Vietnam Vet on the verge of a breakdown? Did he really only get off dressed up in women's lingerie? Had he ever committed murder?

"No, no, Bunny," he said, and took me in his arms, kissed my nose, and ran the tip of his tongue along my eyelashes.

Weekdays I'd rise early while Blase was still buzzing and snorting in bed. His snores were sometimes deep rattlings, sometimes squeaky vibratos, always at a window-rattling volume; sometimes he'd tell people it was due to a hole blown through his septum by pure-grade Peruvian flake, but with me he'd insist he was still suffering the consequences of a broken nose given him in his youth by a big, nasty bully. Blase never seemed capable of deciding whether to pose as dangerous character or hapless victim, so he'd alternate between them, shifting to other personae as the need arose. As I was saying, weekdays I'd rise early and dash to school, where I would drag students through the basics of propositional logic, advancing toward first-order predicate calculus, sympathizing with their "But what good is all this?" questions, wondering if there were something immoral in encouraging students down a path I was vaguely considering abandoning myself.

"A clear example of a valid argument," I'd say. "First premise: If it's raining, the streets are wet. Second premise: It's raining. Conclusion: The streets are wet."

A student in the front row raised her hand.

"But couldn't it rain without the streets' being wet? I mean, suppose they're all covered with tarps? Or suppose the town only has underground streets?"

"Fine," I said. "Let's suppose that. That just makes the first premise false; the argument's still valid. Remember, validity in an argument just means that *if* the premises were true, the conclusion would *have* to be true. Or, put another way, an argument is valid if and only if it's not possible for the premises to be true while the conclusion's false."

I turned to the blackboard and began writing:

If pigs can fly, then I'll be happy.
Pigs can fly.
Therefore, I'll be happy.

From the back of the room, someone yelled, "That's stupid."

"Yes," I said, feeling stupid, "this argument is stupid. The antecedent of the first premise and the entire second premise are silly and obviously false. But the argument's also valid. Which goes to show you just what validity amounts to: a really low standard for evaluating arguments."

My students stared at me and I stared back until

someone said, "If logic only gives us validity as the standard for rating arguments, and it's a really low standard, then what's the use of logic?"

As I searched for ways to lure them back, to make them believe in logic as providing serious objective evaluative criteria, students began closing folders, stacking books, unzipping backpacks, putting on jackets.

A boy in the second row looked at me kindly and said, "Class is over."

Students began to leave their seats, shuffle toward the door, and I said loudly, "One final point." Everyone stopped. "If logic only gave us validity, then, given it's such a low standard, we might be justified in asking, 'What's the use of logic?' But logic gives us other, higher standards—soundness, for example. An argument is sound if and only if it's valid and has true premises. In a few weeks, we'll discuss using *that* to assess arguments."

Someone said, "Far out!" and a few people laughed and everyone was in motion again.

In the evening I'd return from school feeling that, despite my walking down and up the island, despite my hours of meticulous toil and research, I had gone nowhere and that's just where I could expect all these efforts to take me in the long run—nowhere—and I'd find Blase sipping a drink, having put in a good day's work on the Fitzgerald biography, dreaming big optimistic dreams of wealth, success, and fame.

I almost resented having to put so much into something I now considered labor, while Blase stayed home and did what he most wanted to do, but I never said anything. I kept reminding myself I had to be patient: my turn would come. Maybe I'd go into another field, something with real-world currency. Maybe I'd be able to make a positive difference in the world. And Blase would encourage and support me.

Besides, we were young and happy and everything was open to us. The world was an endless web of possibilities. Everything was simple, those days. We were poor, just getting by, and our financial limitations imposed neat, inflexible boundaries on how we could and did spend our time. We took walks along the river, dreamed about our future together. We talked about our rambling old colonial in New England, sheepdogs and children romping through tall fragrant meadows, a vegetable garden and flowering fruit trees. Sometimes we rented videos—we'd gone through all of Hitchcock and Capra and Cukor. Most nights we'd just stay home and read out loud to each other; we'd made it through three Wodehouses, two Waughs, and had just begun *The Shorter Pepys*. On weekends we hung out at galleries in the village, or at the MOMA or the Met, and Blase, who'd studied a lot of art history, made interesting, insightful comments on obscure works we'd discovered together. "This Miró," he'd say. "Does it remind you of anything? Keith Haring, maybe?" We browsed in Second Avenue antiques shops, attended free concerts and readings in Central Park and downtown. Being young, in love, and in New York could really make you feel you stood a chance.

We saw a lot of Claire and David; sometimes we'd have sushi at Claire's orn meatballs at David's, but mostly they came over and we ate pasta and salad, told stories, played games like backgammon and Gomaku.

After our wedding, Blase took to calling me "Bunny," apparently a term of endearment and certainly a safe bet, in case he couldn't remember my name when trying to summon it on the spur of the moment and to protect against accidentally calling me Linda or Rhonda, the kinds of names he used to date.

It was eleven full months before everything was unpacked and I could begin to answer all the questions that Blase was asking, would forever ask, all the way up till the end of our marriage and even beyond: "Where's the phone?" "Where're my keys/sunglasses/wallet?" "Where's the escrow statement from last year?" "Where are the things you promised to send me?"

The day I finally, temporarily found a place for this and that, located and sorted all the bills and correspondence and tiny scraps of paper on which Blase had scribbled telephone numbers, names, addresses, dates, or sometimes just a word or phrase—"ashes and millionaires," "Rayner," "up-and-coming"—I saw a note that said "Sweet Bunny" on the front and opened it, since I was Sweet Bunny.

Thursday afternoon—such a treat! Just that very word—Thursday—will never mean the same to

> me. It will always feel smooth and moist, smell of
> honey, taste of mango. Darling Bunny, what was
> it you put in my ear?

At least I thought I was Sweet Bunny. I rooted through the box, found more notes to Sweet Bunny and three from S.B., each in a different hand. The first was a poem, I guess, and simply said, "I love you, honey. From your Bunny." The second, in a flowery backhand, thanked him for the roses, the pearls, and the fruit basket. Longer, and grammatically more daring, the third note contained an interesting P.S.: "I don't know what a muse is, but I'd be happy to be your one."

Blase was upstairs, in his dark, tiny study working on the Fitzgerald biography. I could hear the clang-clang of the little alarm clock toy he'd bought, the whiz of the tiny sports car. At some point Blase decided that filling the space between thoughts with the external motions of these toys sparked internal motions of the mind, so he was always coming home with a new windup toy; when he was hard at work, I could hear ding-dings and whiz-bangs all the way down-stairs, which, like a child's singing the same song over and over, quickly lost its charm.

"Blase," I began, "these are *yours*." I was holding the box full of his scraps. Chattering teeth slid across his desk. "Where do you want them?" I didn't say "darling" or "sweetheart." I wanted him to know I was pissed off.

"Do you realize Fitzgerald had wanted to call *The Great Gatsby* 'Among Ash Heaps and Millionaires'?"

"No," I said, eyeing that scrap in the box. "Where do you want these?"

"Also, 'Under the Red, White and Blue,'" he said. "Sounds like one of those songs they made you sing in fourth grade."

"Can I put it next to your desk?"

"But these are the best: 'Gold Hatted Gatsby,' 'High Bouncing Lover,' and 'High Bouncing Gatsby.'" He chuckled, wound the kangaroo. "Shows you how important a title is." Then he saw me holding the box and added, "Can you put that next to my desk?" Whiz-plop.

"Blase, I think I've figured out the last three problems: if we pay half on the credit card bills, then we can cover the phone—"

"I'm thinking I'll call it *A Dark Night of the Soul*." Blase straightened a paper clip and skewered the tip of a pencil's eraser.

"Good. Really, that's great," I said. "Plus we'll have enough left over for next month's rent—"

"In *The Crack-Up* Fitzgerald says, 'In a real dark night of the soul it is always three o'clock in the morning.' Of course, these days it's six o'clock, but the sentiment holds." He twisted the little knob on the alarm clock, then the one on the teeth. Ding-ding. Clack-clack.

"And it looks like, if we don't buy those repulsive Japanese prints, we'll actually have enough to repay your mom and dad and maybe even eat out once or twice."

"And the epigraph will be a modification from

141

Fitzgerald's notebooks—it'll go: 'Show me a hero and I'll show you a tragedy.' " He watched the toys zipping around on his desk. Clang-clang. Whiz-zoom. Clatter-clack. He stuck a wad of paper on the end of the paper clip, twirled the pencil between his fingers.

"Blase, are you listening to me?"

"Of course not," he said. "This is very important, Toby. This is My Work."

"Looks to me like you haven't written a word except for the title and the epigraph." It was odd: Blase had begun this work almost a year before, and this was all I'd actually seen of it.

"Yeah—the two most important parts of the book!"

I claimed that the importance of the title and epigraph wasn't as parts of the book because, I said, they *weren't* parts of the book, let alone essential parts, and Blase insisted I didn't know what I was talking about since I wasn't a writer, like him, and I reminded him I'd written at least as many short stories as he had and none of mine ended, "Then the alarm clock rang—it was only a dream," and he suggested something about apples and oranges, and I stuck out my tongue and he kissed it. And thus we ended our discussion of the Sweet Bunnies.

Blase cupped his cheek in his hand and said, "You know, Bunny, Fitzgerald and I are a lot alike."

"Oh, yeah?"

"Yeah. We both went to Princeton, both stunk at football, both wrote a play there, both joined the army—"

"You didn't join the army, Blase," I said.

"Yeah, but they almost drafted me," he replied. "We both worked in advertising—"

"When did you work in advertising?"

"When I wrote for that paper in Newark."

"That was *journalism*," I said.

"Journalism, advertising, same thing," he said. "And we both have beautiful, crazy wives."

"I'm not crazy," I said. Who was I to argue with "beautiful"? "Don't forget Claire and David are coming for dinner, okay?"

"Okay."

The living room/dining room didn't yet have much by way of adornments, just a living urn plant I'd brought from my former life, which, I was amazed to see, had sprouted a baby, a fresh, tender green little vase. A good sign. A very good sign.

Claire arrived first, carrying a bowl of silk apples, plums, pears, oranges, kiwi, bananas, and cherries. "I know how much appearances matter to Blase," she said, "and I figured that with this, at least you'll never *look* like you're going hungry."

I went to tell Blase to hurry up, Claire was here, and he raised his hand, and said, "What do you think: *A Dark* Night *of the Soul* or *A Dark* Morning *of the Soul*—after all, three A.M. *is* morning. For that matter, so is six."

"*A Dark* Night *of the Soul.* Now come on."

David was already there when I got back downstairs, and he and Claire were sitting on the love seat that had come with the place. Looking like she was trying not to laugh, Claire was snorting rhythmically behind a tiny hand, saying, "I can't believe it. Did you make out a police report?"

"Nah," David said, shifting back in the love seat and shaking his head and laughing too. "You think the NYPD's gonna take her in? They'd cuff *me*, undoubtedly, for sexual assault or impiousness or for having such an enticing head."

"What happened?"

"I'm at the corner of Forty-seventh and Second waiting for the light to change," David said, "when all of a sudden I feel pain. At the back of my head. I mean, I'm standing there, and out of nowhere, I'm thinking, *Shit! Something dental is happening to me. Someone's biting my head!* And I turn around and it's a goddamn *nun*! And she's wearing this green sweatshirt over her habit that says 'Be Good to Your Mother' and grinning like a jack-o'-lantern—I mean with only a few big, square teeth, too. And she's carrying a pink balloon."

"The devil's mark," I said. Since my wedding, balloons would never be innocent latex spheres enclosing portions of air. As a child I'd never really cared for them, or for soap bubbles, on which they must have been modeled. Though you could glimpse rainbows and smeary iridescent images sliding on their surfaces, soap bubbles never lasted long enough to really spark dreams or take you away from the world, and as soon as one was within your grasp, all you were holding was a sticky little puddle. Funny, while their lack of substance was what charmed, it was also what disappointed.

"What'd you do?" I said.

"What could I do? I'm wanting to bite her back—but a nun?"

"At least you could have popped her balloon," Claire said.

Finally Blase came down, showed surprise that David and Claire were there, said, "Hey, why don't you guys stay for dinner?" and Claire and I went to make the pasta and let David run through his story again. From the kitchen, I could hear Blase hayekking as if from far away and it made me sweat.

"This is great," Blase said, meaning the pasta was hot and the clams were cooked and we were well into our second bottle of cheap red so that even it was beginning to taste good.

"Y'ever met a writer who's s'posed to be a big shot and it turns out you've never read his stuff—you've never even heard of the guy?" David said.

"You bet," Blase said.

"Sure," I said.

"Yep." Claire nodded.

"Well," David said. "I met this guy at a party last night and—this is what a sonofabitch I am—the guy says he's Robert Something, wrote some book called *Death Before Dawn*, I think. Of course, I've never heard of him, but I say, 'No kidding!' and he says, 'You read it?' and I say, 'You bet! It was great.' And the guy smiles and says, 'Glad you liked it.' Then, when I see him a little later, I could just let it go, right? But I've had a few and I'm feeling pretty generous so I say, '*Some* book!' 'You really think so?' the guy says. 'Yeah,' I say. 'It was even better the second time.' "

We all laughed and Blase said, "Hey, I *read* that book."

"No kidding? Was it any good?" David asked.

"To quote Hobbes, it was 'nasty, poor, brutish and short.' "

David laughed and Claire said, "Sounds like the guy I'm seeing."

Everyone half-truthed and lied and one-upped their way through dinner and a cognac and we were all reclining on the floor by the end of the night, listening to soft, slow jazz.

"Okay, now we're going to play Wish," Claire said. "This magic fairy comes down from the heavens and says—"

"Thith plathe ith a *meth*," Blase said in fake-gay.

"Ha, ha," Claire said. "The fairy—or angel, for the three-year-olds here—says, 'Everybody gets one wish, right now. Only one. And you have thirty seconds to decide what it'll be.' "

David said, "I wish I could put that nun in a muzzle."

"That's your wish?" Claire said.

"Nah, I wish I had a smart, sweet, honest gal who'd call me Daddy and let me tie her up sometimes."

Claire said, "I wish I had a billion dollars."

"Crass materialist," David said.

"No, you could solve a lot of other people's problems with a billion dollars."

"But you wouldn't," David said. "You'd become sneaky and greedy and jealous of it just like all the stinking rich."

"If she wants a billion dollars," Blase said, "she gets a billion dollars. Them's the rules," and suddenly I remembered playing this game as a kid.

It was Christmas, and Mom made us go around the table and say our wishes. As I recall, I wished for a typewriter and Iz wished for two horses, in case one died. Then Anne said, "I wish for peace on earth." I remember that because it was so hokey and because it was so sweet and because it was the spark that lit that Christmas's conflagration. It was just like Anne to wish for peace on earth. She really meant it. And Mom said, "You can't wish for *that*," and Anne said, "Why not? You said we could wish for anything we wanted. That's what I want."

"No you don't," Mom said.

"Yes I do," Anne said.

"Oh, come on, Anne," Mom said. "You *do not* wish for *peace on earth*. You wish for new clothes or a car or a boyfriend. Not *peace on earth*." Anne insisted that's what she wanted, *really*, but Mom laughed at her snidely and when Anne started crying, she called her a fool and moved on to Kate. Anne ran from the table, grabbed the car keys, and drove off in the snow, even though she was wearing slippers and only had a learner's permit. Mom sent the police after her and when they phoned to say they'd caught up with her, Mom said, "Why don't you hold her there for a while? Maybe she'll learn something." And all that time, Dad said nothing and just moved slowly like an old man when we went to take down the Christmas tree. That's what all those Christian holidays were like when I was a kid. No wonder I've always wished I were Jewish.

"I want to sell truckloads of books and be famous," Blase said.

"That's *two* wishes," David said.

"It's *one*," Blase insisted, "a conjunctive wish. I don't want one without the other."

"Claire?" David said.

"Okay, he gets the wish."

Then it was my turn and I said, "World peace," though I really wanted to say, "A baby," and no one laughed and David even said, "That's a good one."

These days, my interest in parenthood seemed to be rising in direct proportion to the waning of my commitment to my work. Often I'd find myself staring at a tiny pink infant who would catch me in an eye-lock from which I couldn't escape until I'd cooed, "How are *you*?" What was funny was that, as I was staring at the babies, checking them out, they stared at me, like the Andover admissions officer, wondering, *Are you really up for this?*

For the most part I thought this baby lust was purely hormonal. But there were other times, times when I could see the roots of the fantasy extended deep into my heart.

"And the biography," David said, "how's it coming?"

"Great," Blase said. "Really great. Just a few little obstacles—"

"Yeah, like *writing* it," I said and everyone laughed but Blase gave me one of those if-looks-could-kill looks you hear so much about but hardly ever see outside of the movies, unless you know my mother, and I leaned over and kissed him and Blase smiled and kissed me back.

"Do you know what you're gonna call it?"

"*A Dark Night of the Soul,*" Blase said, checking David's and Claire's reactions, and they both said it was wonderful, kind of enigmatic and tragic and they'd buy a book with that title in a hot second, and Blase seemed very pleased.

"How 'bout you, Toby," David said. "How's the truth biz?"

"In short? Weary, stale, flat, and unprofitable—which is to say, The Usual," and I felt like a bore so I added, "But I just finished a short story and I'm thinking of sending it out, maybe."

"*Two* writers in the family?" David said. "Toby, I didn't know you'd become a penster."

"She's not really interested in writing per se," Blase said. "It's just this little therapeutic gig she's doing—you know, a little autobiography, a little self-exploration..." and I suppose he was right. Having been raised in a world in which truth was defined by the skewed perceptions of two well-oiled individuals so that I was constantly assured that things weren't as I perceived them, I didn't really have the feelings I thought I had, and now being married to someone who viewed truth in terms of possibility, so that what might have been the case was as sturdy and solid and real as what actually was the case, I was left with constant doubts about the accuracy of my own perceptions and the reasonableness of my emotions. Telling a story gave me a way of shaping events into equations and people into variables and constants so that what happened made sense and even carried a certain deductive weight, as if life were anything like that.

"And I've just sent out my Christmas cards," I said, feeling enthusiastic and ridiculous at the same time, since I never told anyone but Blase about my cartooning.

"What is it, June?" Claire said. "Lord, Toby, you *are* the definition of anal retentive—or is it obsessive-compulsive?"

"Obsessive-compulsive," Blase said. "But Toby's talking about these little cartoons she does—pretty cute, really." He reached over and stroked my calf. "I'm very proud of her," he said, as if I were a little child catching on to toilet training. "She's really quite brave, you know—just sent a batch out to that greeting card company, you know the one, Cute Cards."

"It's Sweet Sentiments, Blase," I said.

"Yeah, right," he said. "Whatever."

"Can we see one?" Claire said.

"This is my favorite," I said, showing them this:

Ho, Ho, Ho!

"Which isn't to say it's technically the best. I just love thinking about thinking, and the thoughts of children."

"Kind of appealing, isn't it?" Blase said, and David and Claire went on rather too much about how wonderful it was and how talented I was and Claire

151

even went so far as to suggest I do Blase's book jacket, which made Blase hayek.

When we got in bed that night Blase was restless, kicking a foot back and forth under the covers, shifting from side to side.

"Something bothering you?" I said.

Blase sat up, turned on the light, and faced me. Then he leaned forward, leaned toward me, put both hands on my shoulders. He cleared his throat. "Toby," he began, "there's something I've got to tell you."

He paused.

I felt a twist in my stomach and suddenly saw Blase in bed, this bed, tossing around with a nameless, faceless, Other Woman. I began to tremble. *So soon*, I thought. *We've been married for a year and already he has something to tell me.* Christ! We were still newlyweds, still belonged to that group of people who were supposed to be tenderly exploring the new, open terrain of another's body, of another's heart and soul.

Blase took a deep breath.

I took a deep breath.

"Bunny, after a year of going nowhere with it, I've decided to give up on the biography."

"Huh?"

"I've decided to write a novel."

I hugged him. "You're kidding!" I said. "That's great!"

"It is?" he said. "Don't you think I'm a quitter, a loser?"

"Of course not," I said.

"Aren't you worried I'll just give up on this, too?"

"No," I said. "Even if you did—so what?"

"Well, I finally realized that just because you love something doesn't mean you can understand its source—I mean, just because I love your mom's cooking doesn't mean I could understand your mom."

I was shocked. "You love my mom's cooking?"

"I was just saying *for example.*"

And this was the very beginning of Blase's first novel, *A Dark Night of the Soul.* Nothing would ever be the same again.

SEVEN

A Dark Night of the Soul

Things changed, as things often change: not suddenly, not so you'd ever think, *Things are changing*, but gradually, in minute increments, so as to be entirely imperceptible, as when the boy becomes a man or winter becomes spring, almost as if it all happened behind your back or when you were out of town or while you were looking the other way, so that you are astonished one day to find yourself thinking, *Things have changed*.

Suddenly I noticed that Blase had adopted a new pose: his food now included hearty beef and potatoes and red wine, lots of red wine, and the day was always capped with snifters of cognac. Briefly he took up a pipe but he must have decided that would better suit a poet or a scholar because he switched to Camel straights. He still sported Brooks Brothers, but he refused to match socks or to let me iron his shirts or pants; he seemed enormously pleased with himself the day he decided to give up socks altogether. And at some point, maybe it was around chapter six, "Limos

Like Black Sharks," Blase began to speak of himself as a serious writer, a *real* writer, and told me I was wise to have invested in him, as if he were a stock soon to split or something, which he sort of was. Sometimes he even spoke of himself in the third person.

Breakfast time, we'd slug down cups of coffee and tea together, ask, Would this man drink Chock Full o' Nuts? And hey, Blase might note, how 'bout *that* as a chapter title? According to Blase, chapter titles were very important, almost of the rank of epigraphs.

"More tea?" I might ask, and add hot water to his cup.

"Wow," Blase might say. "You offer me more *tea*, but you give me more *water*. Wouldn't that be a cool detail to add to the book—you know, nothing's what it seems, you want one thing and get another, and plus, I think it would help advance the plot in chapter four, you know—the one we're calling 'Breakfast at Tiffany's.'"

"You promised to rethink that one," I'd say.

"I will," he'd say. "I am. How 'bout 'Vendor in the Night'? Or 'This Side of Jersey'?"

Blase fretted quite a lot about slang terms. "'Coke,'" he'd say, "sounds like the soda. 'Blow,' 'toot,' 'snow,' and 'powder' all sound like teenage jargon. And 'booze'—so forties. 'Hooch' is Prohibition and definitely comes from stills, though it might have its moment when the guy meets up with that Mafia kingpin. 'Drinks' is too vague, 'cocktails' brings us to the twenties, 'firewater' is Native American."

"What about 'liquor' and 'alcohol'?"

"The first sounds obscene, which I like, but the second rings of laboratories and hospitals, don't you think?"

Every night when I got home from school, Blase would be waiting in the living room, like a little kid with a fistful of papers at the end of his day at school, waiting to show me what he'd written. The first two chapters were so funny and upbeat, I made very few comments that weren't compliments. But the next few chapters left me with the feeling that what I was hearing was more than just fiction. In chapter three, "The Importance of Seeming Earnest," the man seduces two of his students in exchange for As; in chapter four, the man gets drunk, skips out on his class, picks up a limo, a prostitute with a harelip, and the clap, in that order; then in chapter five, *Les Mains Sales,* the man is fired from his teaching position for failure to meet his classes and spends a solitary evening in a bar, crying into his vodka, feeling a failure. Toward the end of the chapter, the man is still leaving his apartment every morning, kissing his wife good-bye, and passing the entire day sucking Jack Daniels from a paper bag, slouched on a bench in Central Park, noting that even the old men playing chess have a greater purpose in life than he. Each night, he returns home to his wife, tells her about his day at school, about how it looks like he'll be up for tenure soon, and, after dinner, drinks himself to sleep in front of Johnny Carson, the Eternal Optimist, cheery under the worst of circumstances like bad ratings and expensive divorces. It's all very sad, until chapter seven, "The Snow Man Cometh," when the man rendezvouses with his good pal, an old college buddy named John, tall and built like an aging athlete, an aspiring writer and coke head, who suggests to the man that he wise up and go into business for himself.

"Blase," I said one evening, "how much of this is you?"

"It's *fiction*, honey," he said, and patted my arm. "None of it's *true*."

"Well, you were an English professor and you did get fired and you were a coke dealer and you do have a friend just like the John character and Johnny does cheer you up—"

"But it's not me *now*. Hey, I couldn't possibly draw on that time if it weren't far behind me."

"I thought you said none of it was true."

"It isn't," Blase said. "I'm like Proust. I begin with my life, my experience, but I'm definitely *not* that guy."

Funny, before he had even published, before another living soul aside from me had read any of the words he'd strung into sentences, let alone said anything encouraging about them, Blase was making comparisons between himself and other, famous writers— not the down-side comparisons of the modest, humble, hopeful apprentice, but comparisons that elevated him to the status of "colleague." "I'm like Fitzgerald," he'd often say. Other times he might observe, "I'm like Hemingway," though he didn't think Fitzgerald and Hemingway were at all alike. Blase, according to Blase, was also like Joyce, Salinger, Donleavy, Mailer, Cervantes, and the anonymous author of *Lazarillo de Tormes*.

"This isn't *autobiography*," Blase said, hugging me, then kissing me and adding, "Were you worried about that? That I was that guy?" and he hayekked and stroked my hair and called me "Sweet Bunny" which was intended to be comforting and fundamentally it was. But it also pissed me off.

As I was saying, every evening when I arrived home from school Blase would read me what he'd written. It was almost immediately a ritual. I'd walk in the door at six, he'd have a bottle of red, two glasses, cheese, and crackers waiting on the coffee table. We'd kiss and Blase would be kicking and rocking on the couch, which in this case meant that he couldn't wait to get down to work. Then he'd clear his throat and begin: "He believes he's the type of person . . . " I'd jot down notes as he read since we decided around chapter three that it was too disruptive if I stopped him at each point I found questionable, there being many such points. Still, when he saw me scribble something on the pad, he'd pause and lean over and try to peek at what I'd written. When he'd finish, we'd drink a glass of wine and then it was my turn. Mostly I made nitpicky editorial comments: "In the last sentence of the second paragraph, you use 'type' for the third time in three sentences. You should use at least one 'sort' or 'kind' or something." Or: "He throws the bottle of J and B in the East River at the top of the page, but at the bottom he's swigging from it again." That kind of thing. But there were times when we'd lock horns over a scene or character, times when it might seem to someone peeking in the window like we were actually *fighting*: "The two blond lawyers, both Harvard grads and former Miss Americas, are wearing pink corsets *and* can't resist this guy? That's ridiculous. And really, Blase, it's such a little-boy jerk-off fantasy. Trash it." I guess I could be more than frank; I could be insulting, especially when Blase's work seemed chauvinistic or shallow—I knew in my heart he was capable of better—and Blase would look hurt and we'd have to sit in silence for a minute till I hugged him and said I was sorry and then we could resume.

"I'm having trouble impressing on my students the difference between ambiguity and vagueness," I said one night.

"Huh," Blase said.

"I've gone over it and over it. I've given them examples and still they seem to think the terms are synonymous."

Blase was staring at something behind me. He didn't blink.

"I think I'm losing them."

Blase continued to stare.

"Blase?"

"Huh," he said.

"Are you listening?"

"Yeah."

"What'd I say?"

Blase blinked as if he'd just come to. "What's that?"

I said, " 'What'd I say?' "

"You were talking about teaching," Blase said.

"But what'd I say?"

159

"You asked me if I was listening."

"Before that," I said.

"You said, 'What a day!' You said maybe you weren't cut out for teaching. You asked me what I wanted for dinner."

"*After* that."

"I can't remember *everything* you say, Bunny. Look, I've got a lot on my mind. I'm a novelist, Toby. I'm in the middle of writing a very important book." After that, I rarely talked with Blase about my teaching, and he never asked.

For the next nine months, our apartment was the scene of frantic industry. Pages covered with red, then green, then blue pencil accumulated on the coffee table, the dining room table, our nightstands, the toilet tank. The place was filled with the clicking of typewriter keys, jingles and ring-dings and whiz-bangs. Blase wrote and rewrote. I typed and proofread and line-edited and dragged myself to the classroom, where I posed questions and gestured toward possible solutions which I knew wouldn't work, wondering if I should really study philosophy, if *anyone* should really study philosophy, and whether I was perhaps guilty of corrupting the youth of New York but decided that would be like being guilty of littering at a dump.

" 'Ball' is ambiguous," I said. "One way to see this is to consider a sentence like—" I searched, then I wrote *Mary likes balls* on the blackboard. "S'pose it turns out Mary likes cotillions, but loathes the objects used in soccer, tennis, and so forth. On one reading of the term, the sentence expresses a true proposition, on the other, a proposition that's false."

"What about the third reading?" someone blurted, and everyone laughed.

"Let's try another term, then," I said.

"How 'bout 'head'?" someone yelled, and folders began closing, zippers zipped, people rose, and the polite student in the second row said, "Class is over."

At home I could get things done: working for Blase, plus laundry and cleaning and cooking and keeping track of bills. There, the world was within my control. I had a neat, ordered life that for the most part made sense. I was dedicated to my marriage. I was devoted to my husband. We would remain happy and together forever. I believed in Blase, and I believed in us.

At lunch or between classes, I'd scribble possible subway scenarios or names for characters, I'd try out different endings or ways to get the character out of jail, or out of the dive-bar where he's slam-dancing with the chip-toothed whore with "Resist Me" shaved in her scalp and into the chichi club with the railroad heiress on his arm. Sometimes I'd come up with an idea Blase would love and he'd scoot to the typewriter and say, "Run that by me again."

Other times the line of propriety would shift and Blase would become irritated at my suggestions or comments and say "Toby, it's *my* book," like a little boy who grows tired of sharing when he sees how much fun his playmate is having with his toys, and I'd call his bluff—"Fine, do it yourself"—and huff off and pretend to work on a short story or a cartoon and after a little while he'd come to me sweetly and say he was sorry and what *was* he going to do to get the character out of jail?

Friends would ask about the Book—which was all we called it then—and we'd say little, like, "It's going well," or "It should be done by the end of the month," though sometimes Blase would say, "It's the next *Gatsby*," as if claiming it was so would make it so.

Though I try to live my life as an orthodox rationalist, committed to the sovereignty of the laws of nature and to their exhaustive explanatory power, pooh-poohing ESP, astrology, telekinesis, remote viewing, and so forth, I've found some of my childish beliefs won't conform: shooting stars, heads-up pennies, cracks in the sidewalk have real weight in my life. I never walk under ladders or sleep with my head pointing south or break a chain letter, and I never count my chickens before they hatch. I warned Blase not to do so either.

"People who count their chickens before they hatch act very wisely," Blase said, "because chickens run about so absurdly that it's impossible to count them accurately," and I laughed. But not for the first time, I had the feeling that someone else's words were leaving Blase's mouth.

As summer began to fade into fall the Book was nearing its end, or its birth, and I was ready to leave philosophy. But I didn't want to quit. There were many states of character I was hoping to develop, but being a quitter wasn't one of them. Still, I was twenty-nine now. I had been prodded by the maternity gene or bitten by the stork or whatever it is that suddenly makes you come at the idea of a man planting his seed in your belly and making a tiny new life, a person who will love you unconditionally, at least for a while, at least while he needs you (which is how it always seems to go), a person who could grow into someone you like and of whom you can be proud, someone who will give you a chance to do right what you saw your parents do wrong, and who will probably make you spend endless nights worrying that you just are your mom or dad and you're doing it all wrong again, which you probably are, but perhaps with your own unique style, which should count for something.

While Blase tinkered with the last chapter of the Book, I researched baby names—'Gazelda' struck me as different and original and Blase gave it the nod since, he said, the nickname would be 'Zelda,' a favorite of his. And 'Casimir' or 'Cash' for short if it were a boy. I spent my lunches and breaks browsing in baby boutiques, marveling at the tininess of it all. I watched people carrying babies, observed the different techniques, and made a note to research positions. It wasn't really that I had become enamored with *babies*. Rather, I grew weak in the knees, warm and mushy and passionate over the idea of *my* baby, who would undoubtedly be small and sweet and quiet from the start.

* * *

"What does Blase think?" Claire asked. We were slurping soup at a noodle shop downtown.

"Sometimes he seems to get pretty excited about the idea; other times he says we're not ready for children. He doesn't seem to know his own mind."

"What's to know?" Claire said. She touched the back of my hand. "Hey, I'm kidding. Anyway, regardless of Blase's feelings here, are you sure having a baby now wouldn't just be a way to avoid dealing with your own life?"

"No. I really want a baby."

"Yeah, me too. I sympathize with that. But don't think that having one will solve your questions about yourself and what you should be doing."

"I don't," I said, wondering if I did.

"If you're not happy doing philosophy and teaching, then think about your alternatives. Jesus, Toby, even if you crammed the next twenty years with babies and drool and diapers there'd still come a moment when you'd have to face yourself. Having kids now will just postpone it. I mean, do you really think it'll be *easier* to decide what you want to do with your life and your God-given talents when you're fifty?"

Maybe she's right, I thought, and it pissed me off.

Finally Blase submitted the Book to Cam Warner, an old friend of his father's now at Winston Brothers. Six weeks later, Cam gave it the go-ahead. We hugged each other. We jumped up and down. We skipped around the apartment. Blase made up a song about becoming rich and famous, attaching "Bunny! Bunny!" to the end of each stanza. Then we drank two bottles of cheap champagne down by the river—just like on our first date only it was somehow more magical, less real—and we danced to Blase's rendition of his latest favorite song while he held me tightly and rocked me in his arms, and fell way off key at:

> "I couldn't foresee
> At the age of twenty-three,
> That I'd have pick of the chicks
> When I reached thirty-six."

We sat on a bench and whispered together about the possible size of the advance ("What if they gave me fifty thousand, Bunny!"), about how many copies he might be able to sell ("Imagine if I sold twenty-five thousand! Twenty-five thousand fans!"), about when we might be able to have a baby. "Soon," was all Blase said. "Very soon." Along with the other men I'd known, parenthood and the idea of an actual, living baby didn't seem to have much of an intrinsic positive- or negative-poled magnetism for Blase—though the idea of an heir struck him as charming—while at some point most women I knew went into back flips over the possibility of conception. For some time I attributed this difference to the fact that we little girls were primed for motherhood for years, opening endless packages of hard plastic baby dolls and infants, doll layette sets and toy bottles and diapers and such, until I remembered that we didn't really love the dolls until we'd pulled out their hair and drawn on their faces with blue crayon or yanked off a leg.

For a while we elaborated on our fantasy—the colonial would be in Maine. It would have six bedrooms, an enormous meadow, and our three happy, healthy children would romp through the tall grass, picking wildflowers and playing hide-and-seek—until I realized Blase was utterly silent and I was doing all the elaborating.

We sat quietly, closely, on the bench for what seemed like hours, holding each other and dreaming, until Blase jumped up and began to dance and sing "New York, New York."

"You're in a mood," I said, and I couldn't blame him. Suddenly new roads were suggesting themselves in the vague mist of our futures: Maybe Blase could become a real writer, or a successful writer. Maybe he could support me now and I could leave the nitpicking, backbreaking world of philosophy, write short stories, or actually sell my cartoons. Maybe I'd go to law school or perhaps I'd become an editor. Regardless, it was possible that now we could have a baby, start a real family. But these were my dreams. From this distance I can assure you that Blase saw it all quite differently: his name splashed across the front page of the *Daily*'s Sunday Book Review and beneath it, the rave of raves. Hundreds, thousands, nondenumerably many beautiful fans pasting his face with red and pink and mauve kisses, offering him gifts, loving him, calling, chanting, screaming his name; money, luxury, fame.

"Bunny, what say we head down to the Dinky and score a little blow?"

"What?"

"It's a celebration," Blase said. "Not every day you get a book accepted by Winston Brothers. Please?"

I felt guilty for saying it, but I said okay as long as we could take a cab, since I was feeling lazy, which we could since Blase was feeling rich. I figured that maybe doing coke, for Blase, could be a once-in-a-great-while deal, the kind of crazy thing you do when the world tilts and, for a few moments, you're on top. First we had to go home so Blase could call Everyone and thrill them with the good news.

Just as when we became engaged, Blase tried to phone anyone he even vaguely knew, but it was Friday night, and no one was home, except for my mother and a few maître d's who were down on their luck. And though they were delighted, ecstatic, it wasn't exactly what Blase had been looking for. That night, Blase was looking for a big buzz. Later that's what he'd look for most nights. But there was something more than the coke and the crowd, something else, that always seemed to elude him, that powered him out into the night, into noisy, garish clubs with shallow beautiful strangers, something more, I thought, than flattery and free drugs and the incessant, insistent pawing of anonymous admirers trying to capture a bit of starlight.

So he phoned Jib and Jib said he was on his way out, couldn't talk, but Everyone would be at the Ingenue and didn't Blase want to come, and of course Blase did, said we'd meet Jib there later, after we took care of "some business."

Walking into the Dinky was like walking into any working man's bar in America: there was a pool table, two dart boards, a pinball machine, old tin advertising signs for tobacco and soda pop on the walls, a long oak bar with high stools on which were perched a variety of beer-drinking, T-shirted laborers in various stages of inebriation—which is to say, it was a real anomaly in New York and not the sort of place Blase would hang out in, now or later, if it weren't for the special powder hiding in tiny envelopes and glass vials in people's pockets.

Blase and I climbed on bar stools and ordered beer.

"No one's here," he said and I felt decidedly relieved until a hand slapped his back, making him spill beer from his raised glass all over his face and the counter and his jeans.

"Hey, sport. Should've known I'd find you here, swilling at the Dust Shop." Jib slapped Blase's back again. "Heard some yapping today up at my editor's—did Warner really take the book?"

"You bet." Blase seemed so casual about it, like he'd published a thousand books already so why not one more?

"Then it's party time," Jib said, eyeing the door. "And look who just blew in."

Blase and Jib ducked off to the men's with Tumbleweed, the Dinky's resident dealer, leaving me alone at the bar, apprehensive and a little frightened sitting under the hungry stares of drunken laborers.

Five minutes.

"Hey, doll." Pouches under the eyes. Unshaven. Dirty nails. Bad breath. A T-shirt splattered with red and black paint. "Buy you a drink?"

Seven minutes.

No front teeth. Hand on my waist. Eyeballs barely held in their sockets by bright red nets. Bad breath. "I never seen you here before."

I stared at my hands. I picked my nails, scratched at my cuticles. Pretended I was thinking about something pressing and important.

Twelve minutes. And there was Blase—already glassy-eyed, sniffling, and gritting his jaw. "I wouldn't call it rocket fuel," he said, "but maybe I'll just have to run a few more tests."

Blase took my arm and hurried me into the men's, a tiny space the size of a closet with peeling paint and a hole chiseled into the plaster above the toilet. Jib was throwing his head back, inhaling deeply when we entered. On the wall where a mirror should have been, someone had penned: "What's another word for 'thesaurus'?" Blase pointed at it and laughed. " 'Nomenclator'? 'Repository'?" I said and he frowned. Then Blase showed me how to make a fist and leave a small indent at the base of my thumb. He smiled and kissed my cheek and sprinkled some coke into the depression.

The cab slid across two lanes and pulled up to the curb in front of the Dinky.

"Hot dog!" Blase said.

"Yes, it's a Checker," Jib said, opening the rear door, "the white man's guerdon."

Blase patted the roof. "Wanna ride up here?"

"Up there?"

"You know—have a view of the city, be home-coming queen."

I laughed, but he put his hands on my waist, lifted me on top of the cab.

I tried to slide off but Blase kept pushing me back, insisted we have a little fun, until the cabbie, wielding a baseball bat, convinced him he was being an asshole.

The Ingenue was the brand new, lavishly appointed club for the beautiful people, who, it seems, needed a new club every month, which is about how long it took the ugly people to discover it and tarnish it with their presence. Unlike in the days of the El Morocco and the Coconut Grove, the entrances to exclusive clubs were always hideous—rusted doors, no signs or glittery lights or tongues of red carpet to welcome you and lure you in. The only intimation of luxury was the plush crimson cord marking the boundary between In and Not In, so a certain amount of faith was required just to enter.

"Jameson promises this place is rube-proof," Jib said, ducking out of the cab.

The line of choose-me's was composed of the most exquisite of the beautiful people: women in skinny black dresses with their hair and makeup just so, leaning into men in rich Italian suits with silk ascots, all made by designers whose names Jib would know, who had on their faces expressions that said, *Hey, she's nothing—I have over a dozen at home just like her.* And Blase was trying to shove me across the seat of the cab, toward the door, out on the sidewalk, and into this crowd of the confident, the elite, and the fair.

"I don't—" I began.

"Bunny, if you don't want to come in, I'll just send you home," he said.

"Don't call me 'Bunny,' " I said.

"Yeah, why don't we do that? You look awfully tired." Blase kissed my cheek, exited onto the street, and gave the driver our address and money.

"That guy," the cabbie said, "you're better off without him. No offense, but he's gotta be mental— putting his woman on top of a cab?" The driver looked at me in the rearview mirror. "Plus, leaving somebody like you on a Friday night?" He shook his head. "Shucks."

I shrugged.

"Your boyfriend?"

"My husband."

"Sorry."

As the cab pulled off, I saw Blase and Jib edging into the group, shaking hands and kissing cheeks, as if these were people they knew and trusted, people they belonged with; by the time we stopped at the next corner for the light, I couldn't see Blase. There was simply a crowd of ordinary people anxious for something extraordinary to happen.

* * *

Lying alone in bed that night, waiting to hear the sounds of Blase stumbling around downstairs, or the frantic ring of the alarm clock or the phone, I tried to figure out why he wanted to do coke— he'd said he'd had enough of it, agreed it was a waste—but my thoughts kept drifting into shiny, noisy clubs filled with a crowd of beautiful strangers surrounding Jib and Blase, and Blase's voice, "*Now* we're having fun."

Four o'clock. I smoked a cigarette. Read Twain's "Thirty Thousand Dollar Bequest."

I was pacing the bedroom at four forty-six, thinking about phoning Claire, who would simply tell me I knew about this side of Blase before I married him, which would be the equivalent of "I told you so" and not exactly what I needed at the moment.

Four fifty-eight. Maybe I would phone Iz, who would blame everything on New York.

Five-oh-five. I switched off the light, but I could still see the insistent glow of the numbers on the clock. I lay on my side. I lay on my stomach. I stared at the clock again.

Five-twelve. The back of my neck was clammy; I was grinding my teeth, which I decided to brush.

Five twenty-two. The person I really wanted to talk with was my mother, as if she could somehow make it all right, or at least offer the words that would soothe and lull my heart into a calm, even beat. Fantasies, I realized, once ingrained, can become as unyielding as habits, showing themselves in our behavior as inexorable dispositions, stubborn expectations.

Why did I persist in thinking that when I phoned *my* mom, I'd somehow get Leave It To Beaver's mom? My mom wouldn't serve me something cozy and kind like mashed potatoes, something like, "Boys will be boys" or "This too will pass." She'd say, "That cad! I knew it! I'll be right there," and hop on the next plane. She'd try to convince me to come back and live with her, but I'd insist everything was okay, really, I was just upset, this never happened before, etc., and reluctantly she'd return to Massachusetts, never able to forgive Blase—or me, for denying her this chance to take center stage. I brushed my teeth again.

Five-thirty.

"Alex?"

"Who is it?"

"It's Toby."

"Toby?"

"I woke you. I'm sorry. It's just that we never got to talk at the wedding—"

"What time is it?"

"Four-thirty, your time."

"What's wrong?"

"Nothing. I was just thinking about you and, you know, how we never got to talk at the wedding, and—"

"Shit, Toby! What: you're just sitting around at five-thirty on a Saturday morning and it suddenly dawns on you that we didn't get to talk a year, a year and a half ago, so you phone me now for a chat?"

"No." I wanted to tell her it was Blase, or my marriage, but I was held back by the fear that *saying* these were problems would somehow make them

173

problems. Besides, maybe I was really unhappy about something else. Maybe it was my work. "I guess I was lonely."

"Where's Blase?"

"Asleep."

"Why don't you wake him? Maybe something's bothering you that you two could work out together." God, I loved Alex. It was like the woman had emotional radar.

"Good idea," I said.

"Unless there's something else, something you can't talk to him about."

"Oh. No," I said. "Nothing like that."

"Why don't you do that, then? Wake Blase and talk with him, okay? And then call me back tomorrow. I'll be in all day."

"Great."

"Toby, are you okay?"

"Fine. Just can't sleep."

"Well, make sure to call me tomorrow, all right?"

"Sure.".

"Good. B'bye."

" 'Bye."

"Hey, Toby," she said, "I miss you too," and hung up.

Five forty-five.

I went downstairs, dug a pack of cigarettes from my purse. Blew smoke rings until I thought I'd pass out.

Five fifty-six.

"Mom?"

"What? What happened?"

"Nothing. I just couldn't sleep."

Silence.

"Have a brandy."

"I don't think so." Liquor did not, at this point, strike me as the particular panacea of which I was in need.

"Take a Valium."

Silence.

"You *do* have Valium, don't you? I told you you should always have Valium on hand, for times like this."

"Thanks, Mom."

Then it was six o'clock. Where was my husband? Busted and cuffed in the back of a police car? Holding a spoonful of magic dust under the dainty nostrils of a frosted Lycra lady? Caught in the cross fire of a Mafia hit? Clutching his chest, dying of a heart attack on the floor of a nightclub? Not at home. Not at home in bed with me.

This will never happen again, I thought, as if it were somehow going to be up to me.

Later that morning I went to the supermarket to get chocolate milk, the only thing Blase could stomach on a hangover. I took phone messages from his father and Jib, canceled his lunch date with Cam Warner. Blase hadn't stumbled in till seven A.M. and I'd let him have it—"Where have you been?" "How could you?" etc., though really, part of me was jealous that he had chosen to play with Jib instead of me—and now I was feeling guilty.

The advance turned out to be $8,500, not bad, we consoled ourselves, but not exactly the stuff for ransoming kings or moving up in the world, either, Blase said. Still, this wasn't about money, it was about Art, and Blase was actually going to be allowed to make a contribution to it by way of offering to the public *A Dark Night of the Soul*. "Besides," he added, "the real money comes from royalties."

In May we received our first copies of *Dark Night* and Blase signed one for me.

"This wasn't really necessary," I said.
"Read it," he said.

Dearest Toby,

Whatever becomes of this book, I will always like it better because of its connection with one of the most exciting and important events of my life— starting a new life with you.

All my love,
Blase

I suppose I had expected something different, something more like, "Thanks for all your help."

"Congratulations!" my mom said when she received her copy. "You've had a baby!"

"What's that?" I said.

176

"The book," she said. "It must feel like your child."

Because her main achievement in life had been producing offspring, Mom thought of successes and failures in terms of reproduction. When my ex-boyfriend dumped me for the tiny, well-muscled Karate Monster, Mom said I'd had a miscarriage. When I submitted an article on rigid designators to *Mind*, she congratulated me on my pregnancy, consoled me when it was rejected: "You know what they say about a stillborn—it just wasn't meant to be."

"Which one am I?" Mom said.

"Which what are you?"

"Which character in the book. I'm pretty sure I'm the head of the English Department."

It turned out that quite a few of our friends and immediate family thought they were characters in the book, and most insisted they were the John character—charming, hip, attractive, clever, and immoral in a careless, hedonistic way which spoke to the secret lusts of many.

Finally *A Dark Night of the Soul* began to appear in bookstores around town and reviews began to show up here and there, short reviews shoved in the back pages, mostly, modest reviews containing faint praise: "But Mr. Regenhere may, after all, have some talent." By and large, the critics seemed to find *Dark Night* too sensational, morally questionable, and too thin on plot, though some implied that the writing was interesting or showed promise.

I saved every review, every article mentioning

Dark Night or Blase in a scrapbook. I numbered the pages of the scrapbook, put an index in the front.

Then the phone began to ring. People around the city wanted to meet Blase. They wanted him to come to their parties and drink their booze and nosh on their cocktail wieners and regale their friends with tawdry tales of a glamorous, dangerous subculture. When the time came for him to do his first reading, Blase fretted and stewed about his hair, and I chose the wittiest passages for him to read, the least tattered blazer for him to wear. He came downstairs decked out in rumpled Brooks, his hair gelled straight, packed against his head. He kissed me and said, "I don't suppose you want to come—"

"Of course I want to come," I said.

"It'll be a bore, really. You've heard it all before."

"But I want to be there for you."

"Besides," Blase added, "I'm waiting for a call from an agent. She loves the book and wants to represent me."

"But it's your first reading."

"Really, Bunny, it's important."

Blase kissed me, and hustled out of the apartment. Like the dog left behind by its master, I hurried to the window and watched him walk away, all bowlegged, but a perceptible bounce in his step now. He was whistling.

On the window sill sat the living urn plant. It had sprouted another baby, another soft green tiny pot. I smiled, put my finger in the pot, and stirred.

EIGHT

Days of Lines and Poses

And things changed.

Suddenly, every morning we woke to the phone's ring, people wanting to set up interviews, book signings, readings, and photo shoots, people inviting Blase to their parties, Cam Warner informing us that British, French, and Japanese rights had sold, that two studios were interested in the movie rights. Sometimes it was a breathless fan—"Is Blase Regen-here there?"— wanting to thank Blase for writing such a brilliant book, it was the story of the fan's life, really; "I feel like you followed me around for a month!" the fan might say. Somehow this tale had connected with the real lives of real people all over New York and the book became a Bible and Baedeker for the beautiful people and the social out-of-towners.

As the semester was drawing to an end, I found myself in the unhappy position of being about to flunk fifty percent of my students. I had somehow failed to hammer the basic inference rules of symbolic logic into their heads, so that now they were utterly mystified by and completely unequipped to deal with the predicate calculus. I decided to move on to fallacies. Straw man, begging the question, *ignoratio elenchi*— these were invalid methods of reasoning everyone could get a grip on.

"I don't see why that's a fallacy," a girl said.

I looked at what I'd written on the board.

Einstein claimed that some of the attributes and relations Newton held to be absolute are actually relative.

Therefore, some of the attributes and relations Newton held to be absolute are actually relative.

"Well," I said, "you're probably wondering why it's *fallacious* and not just *invalid*. And that's a good question. Really. We can spend some time on that. But for now, you can see that it's invalid, right?"

"No," the girl said. "The premise is true and I think the conclusion is too."

"Is that sufficient to make an argument valid?" Damn, we were back to this. I turned to the board and wrote:

I am married.
Therefore, I have no children.

"Now, the premise is true, and the conclusion's true, but the argument's not valid. Can you see that?"

Puzzled stares from my students.

"It's possible for the premise to be true—which it

is, as a matter of fact—and the conclusion false. That is, I could be married and have children."

Silence. More puzzled stares.

I turned back to the board, wrote:

$2 + 2 \neq 4.$
Therefore, $2 + 2 = 4$.

"Can anyone tell me if this argument is valid?"

Nothing.

"Please?"

A boy said, "It's invalid?"

"No!" I said, stamping a foot. "The argument's *valid*. Why?"

More silence.

"What's validity?"

Nothing.

Finally a boy raised his hand.

"Yes?"

"Class is over," he said.

My eyes were burning. I turned my back to the students as they packed up and watched my words— *$2 + 2 \neq 4$, I have no children*—blur to a white fuzz on the blackboard.

On my way home from school that evening, I stopped at a bookstore and bought Barron's *How to Prepare for the LSAT*.

From the sidewalk in front of our building I could hear the music blaring. Frank Sinatra crowing about New York. I crossed to the other side of Sixty-third, climbed the stoop of the building facing ours so I could see into our apartment, see Blase doing a little dance-shuffle in the middle of the living room. He disappeared for a moment, then returned to the center of the room with a fluted champagne glass in his right hand. He was facing the mirror on the living room wall, holding the champagne glass like a trophy. His lips were moving and he kept glancing at the champagne glass. Then he bowed slightly and waved to the mirror.

By the time I opened the door of our apartment, Blase was settled on the love seat, thumbing through a magazine. The music had stopped.

"Hey," he said, looking up from the magazine.

I kissed him and smelled liquor.

"Whacha been doing?" I said.

"Most recently I've been reading about the construction of the Holland Tunnel. Nasty business. All that digging and dirt and so forth." He slapped the magazine on the coffee table. "But let's forgo small talk." He rose from the couch and patted the back of a chair. "Sit," he said and hurried off to the kitchen. A few moments later, he reappeared with two glasses and a bottle of champagne, unopened. As he peeled the foil and uncaged the cork, Blase was saying, "So Warner phones and—shit, I really don't think they need these childproof tops on champagne, do you? Well, guess how many copies *Dark Night* sold last week. Go ahead, guess."

"Five thousand?"

Blase filled the glasses and laughed. "Be serious."

"Ten thousand?"

Blase clicked his tongue. "Kid stuff."

"Okay. How 'bout twenty thousand?"

Blase frowned. "Yeah."

I kissed him, squeezed him tight. "Congratulations."

"Only writer who did better last week was Dickens and only because they just released that movie, but he's dead so I figure that doesn't really count."

"Blase, that's fantastic. It means people really like your book."

"More than that, my dear—at a royalty of fifty cents a copy it means ten thousand dollars for us."

I raised my glass. "Congratulations."

After we emptied the bottle Blase ducked out to get another and I headed for the kitchen to see about dinner. The fridge was bare except for a carton of chocolate milk, half a loaf of bread, a couple of weary vegetables and some stiff cheese. The necks of two champagne bottles stuck out of the garbage can.

Halfway through our second bottle of champagne, Blase grew maudlin and began holding forth about the early days of his literary career, days of scrimping and eating cheap food and worrying about the phone bill, as if those days weren't these days. Then he held forth about fiction, saying, "Writing a novel is like driving at night with your headlights on—you can't see very far in front of you, but you can make the whole trip that way." I liked the analogy, I'd heard it before, and I knew it wasn't his.

"No, it's not."

"What?" Blase said.

"Writing a novel is not like driving at night with your headlights on."

"How would you know?" he said.

"Look, with a trip in a car you have a certain destination in mind from the start, right? A precise ending to the journey—even if you're just going for a drive, you plan to end up home, for example. If you don't reach *that* end point, you are what we call 'lost.' I assume that the point about writing a novel is that you don't necessarily have to have any particular ending in mind when you begin. So the analogy fails."

Blase scratched his head and considered. Finally he said, "Why do philosophers always begin their sentences with 'Look'? I hate that."

"Blase, where did those empty champagne bottles come from?"

"Whoa—if you really don't remember, I'm cutting you off."

"Not these bottles," I said, gesturing at the two on the coffee table. "The ones in the kitchen garbage."

"I don't know—where does anything come from? The store, I take it."

"Did you drink them yourself?"

"I may have. Let me think. Ah, yes. I've got it. Warner phoned with the good news and I bought a couple of bottles to celebrate. The first stunk so I poured it out after a mere sip. The second stunk as well."

"You poured them out?"

"Bunny, they were *garbage*. And you know there's only one thing you can do with garbage."

Critics became sensitive to the fact that readers adored the book, and more, and lavish, reviews began to appear in prestigious newspapers and magazines, which had the effect of making *Dark Night* even more of a sensation, which had the effect of making Blase purchase darker sunglasses to let people know that he didn't want to be recognized in public, which he wore on his head, so that someone might recognize him in public, which no one ever did. Not yet, at least. We had to unlist our phone number, but since we were never at home anymore, we had to buy an answering machine. And suddenly there were checks, long pastel-colored checks with lots of zeros. Blase cashed them and went on wild sprees in boutiques downtown and on Madison. He bought suits. He bought shoes, specially ordered a pair of crocodile loafers from Italy, handmade for his stumpy feet. Blase bought silk shirts, dress shirts, easy cotton clothes for relaxing in, a tuxedo and solid gold studs. He bought hats for his big head—which he never wore—ascots, ties, smoking jackets, money clips, silk socks, ostrich accessories. Blase shopped and purchased and rearranged his wardrobe until we looked like a baron and his scullery maid.

So late one afternoon on my way home from school, as I passed Casa de Moda, a boutique whose busy, cheerful windows always gave me pause, a pair of billowy Moroccan wedding pants caught my eye and I entered with a firm intention to buy. The store was loaded with luscious, blousy dresses, jackets, and pants patterned with small flowers and confident batiks from the Caribbean and the Middle and Far Easts, dainty dangly earrings with tiny stones, necklaces threaded with chunks of amber and turquoise, strands of silver twisted and braided into bracelets. A sales-woman zipped and buttoned and snapped and belted and admired and agreed and after two hours, I left the store with a pale pink shopping bag.

"Six hundred dollars?"

"But look what I got! Two silk tank tops, two skirts—"

"Yes, I see. And I'm sure you expect me to say this stuff is nice, but it's not. It's ugly, Toby. You just don't have a sense of style."

The following weekend Blase took me to Italian boutiques with cream carpets, crystal chandeliers, up-holstered chairs around glass coffee tables splattered with glossy magazines, and genuine French provincial armoires each displaying five or six garments. With folded arms, a critic's eye, and a definite sense of what he was looking for, Blase had me walk and turn and bend over and reach up and sit down in narrow dresses with padded shoulders, long silk and wool blazers with padded shoulders, skirts full and narrow, pants with high waists, coats, capes, hats, blouses, boots, shoes, shaking his head or nodding like a silent bidder to the eager salesclerk. He chose velvet dresses, silk dresses, strapless dresses, and to relax in, clingy cotton and Lycra dresses. Then he chose six pairs of pants, three silk skirts, four pairs of Italian heels ("They hurt," I said. "But they look great," Blase said), two pairs of Italian boots, a mink coat, various blazers— short and long, narrow and unstructured—and, all in all, profanely expensive, absurdly trendy clothing, in muted tones of black and grey, clothing I never would have selected myself but which made me look very au courant.

While Blase ushered me up and down Madison making me try on this and that, two people recognized him as someone famous, though the first mistook him for a local weatherman, which pissed him off but he signed the autograph anyway. The second person, a young woman, grabbed his arm and said, "Hey! I know you! You're Blase Regen-here! I *loved* your book—you know, *Soul of Midnight*."

"*Dark Night of the Soul*," Blase said.

"Yeah, right." The woman sank a couple of inches, then bounced up from the knees, saying, "I just *love* you! I mean, I love your book. You're great."

"Thanks," Blase said, shaking her hand and chuckling, and as we walked on he said, "See, Toby? That happens to me *all the time*," as if for him, flattery and fame weren't things he longed for but constituted some enormous burden he had to bear.

WILD, WACKY FUN!
HIGH TIMES ON DARK NIGHTS IN NEW YORK
A TIMELY TALE OF TRAGEDY IN TINSELTOWN
PRINCETONIAN PENS NEW *CATCHER IN THE RYE*

These were some of the headlines appearing in newspapers and magazines around New York and the rest of the country. I cut out each one for the scrapbook, but Blase pasted them on the bathroom mirror and above his desk.

*   *   *

Many perks came with Blase's new position: free tickets to concerts, the theater, and club openings; invitations from famous people to parties that would be covered by *Town and Country*; offers to write articles and columns, to appear on talk shows and even in guest spots on several television series. For reading at a university or arts center, for helping to host a party or penning a few words about tennis shoes, checks the size of my annual salary would appear in our mailbox. A maître d' could always find a table for Blase, and drinks and desserts and sometimes even whole meals would be complimentary. Fewer perks attached to my new position: Blase no longer had time to listen to me relate the details of my day at school. In contrast to his success, my work seemed even more futile and tedious than it had before, when we were both aspiring to be somebody. My professors and colleagues assumed we were rich now and snubbed me, though when Blase showed up at the department one afternoon everyone gathered around him and told him how much they loved *Dark Night* and asked about film possibilities and laughed at his jokes. For months I'd been trying to work up the nerve to discuss my thesis topic with Dr. Harding, who didn't know my name and twice mistook me for a secretary, and there he was, this highly esteemed metaphysician widely reputed to be the crowned prince of Western philosophy, staring open-mouthed at Blase, hanging on his every word as Blase waved his arms and snapped his fingers and exaggerated wildly about the misdeeds of a famous actress at a recent fund-raiser. Outside of the department, no one Blase and I were introduced to remembered my name or what I said I did or even just how I was related to Blase.

"Maybe you should throw yourself at Nietzsche." Della and I were sitting in a coffee shop after school one day. She'd asked about my thesis and I'd told her I was losing interest. "That kind of post-Aristotelian existentialist ethical angst you seem to feel might really be quenched by him."

"I don't know."

"Well, what other questions speak to your essence, as you've defined it?"

"I've always been interested in the mind-body problem," I said. "But I doubt I'll get anyone to work with me on it."

"Why not?"

"Well, I think there really might be souls."

"Jesus, Toby! You don't look like a dualist."

I shrugged. "I've always wanted to try my hand at skepticism." I lit a cigarette. "I used to fret a lot about Wittgenstein's Private Language Argument."

"Was he for or against?"

"Against."

"But what matters to you now?"

"Cosmology," I said.

"Like what?"

Like why I was born, I thought, but that wasn't cosmology. Damn, I was sliding into continental territory, into existentialist concerns, phenomenology, subjectivism. Soon I'd be talking about Being-for and Being-of and wading through the mist onto the shifting ground of deconstructionism and all the nonsense and mumbo-jumbo that went with that. "Like why there's something rather than nothing."

That evening, Blase took me to a new Italian restaurant uptown for an intimate dinner to thank me for all my help on *Dark Night*, he said.

"Couldn't we go to that Indian restaurant?" I said. "The one you first took me to?"

"Are you kidding? Toby, I'd be mobbed by the hoi polloi." Blase's fame had grown, but it was still only the fame of the hometown kid makes good. But maybe because the hometown was New York, and like many New Yorkers Blase thought it was the center of the universe, he believed his name had become a household word. When I'd try to get him to accompany me to the library, a museum, or a gallery, he'd say, "Toby, I'm a famous writer. I can't just go out in public like that," as if his presence would incite a riot. Funny, but he always took that risk at night, when Jib summoned him to a must-come party or club.

When the maître d' of the new restaurant didn't recognize Blase, or his name, simply turned on his heel and led us to a dimly lit table way in the back, near the kitchen, Blase said, "And Warner said this was such a great place? Remind me to change editors."

Blase chose our appetizers and wine and kept straightening up, looking past me, over my head toward the door. "Damn it! Can you believe that? That mongoloid gave Seabury *our* table."

After making the wine steward endure a moment's anxiety while he held the 1959 Côte d'Or in his mouth, raised his eyebrows, then wrinkled his nose, looking like he might spit it out, Blase finally swallowed, said, "Fine. It's fine," and the steward smiled and nodded and filled our glasses.

"To you, darling," Blase said, "the best secretary a guy could have."

Then he handed me a small turquoise box. "Go ahead. Open it."

Diamond earrings. Big old sparkly diamond earrings. The stones on the lobes of every woman in the restaurant, the sort of gift a secretary would select on behalf of her boss who'd suddenly realized it was his wife's birthday.

"Thanks," I said, putting them on.

"They're from Tiffany's."

"Neat."

Then he disclosed their carat weight, the cut, and the fact that he spent quite a while, a good hour, at that store, could have purchased larger, but not better, ones.

I nodded.

"While I was there, I picked this up," he said, pushing back the sleeves on his left arm. A big shiny watch. Gold. A Rolex. A fat cat's watch.

"*Well.*"

Blase stared at his watch for a few moments. "It's really quite practical," he explained.

"I'll bet it even tells time."

"I mean, it's an investment—the best watch made and solid gold. Great resale value."

Was I supposed to be pleased about all this? About his sudden acquisitiveness with regard to blatant, gaudy status symbols? About his apparent show of thoughtfulness in buying me stones reaped from the slave labor of a racist culture when what I'd really wanted, what I'd been begging for for months, was an artist's table?

"Anything wrong?"

"Not really," I said.

"If you want you can get bigger ones," he said, "but they'll be flawed."

"No, they're fine," I said. "Lovely. I was thinking about something else."

"Oh yeah?"

"I had coffee with Della this afternoon and I realized something."

I waited.

Blase took a sip of wine and gazed at his watch.

"I'm going to change my thesis topic," I said.

Blase looked down at his chest, smoothed his tie.

"I'm thinking about writing about something in cosmology."

"Oh yeah?"

"Yeah. Something about explanation and why there's all this stuff. I've heard people argue from the fact that there's all this stuff to the conclusion that there must be a God, a creator. I guess people think, Where did all this stuff come from? Why not just an empty universe? That is, Why is there something rather than nothing?"

"Jesus," Blase said. "I'll bet those people wouldn't be happy even if there *were* nothing."

He wiped his mouth, took a sip of wine, wiped his mouth again, cleared his throat, patted his gelled hair and said, "Bunny."

"Yes?"

"Have you ever heard of Days of the Week?" Of course I'd heard of Days of the Week. Everyone alive during the 1980s had heard of Days of the Week—it was a beauty company whose gimmick amounted to the claim that each person had color tones that went with one of the seven days of the week. Sundays were pinks and creams and beiges, while Thursdays were golds and rusts. Color-blind women all over America had flipped out over the idea of someone telling them what hues to wear, what was guaranteed to make them look like Sophia Loren, and the woman who'd formed the company made millions—until, that is, the woman, an erstwhile Tuesday, had discovered, after careful, objective scrutiny, that she was really a Saturday, and threw herself off the Triboro Bridge.

"Yeah?" I said.

"Well, you're always complaining about how you don't know how to use makeup, so I've made you an appointment with them for next Saturday."

"You're kidding." Of course he was. He couldn't mean it.

"No. Look, I know the stuff about days of the week is absurd, but they're also going to teach you about skin care and about how to apply makeup."

"Blase!"

"I had to send in a photo of you so they'd be able to place your day of the week before you arrive. Really, it'll be helpful."

Suddenly, a big commotion. Lots of confusion. The shaking of hands, the kissing of cheeks, the swapping of names. Then Blase was having me scoot over

and chairs were being brought and busboys were lay-
ing new places, then Blase was pulling back my chair
and hurrying us over to a different table, and I said,
"What's going on?"

"It's Jib," Blase said. "I bumped into him today
and mentioned we were coming here and he said he
might join us." He laughed. "Seems he's brought a few
friends."

Ten. Ten friends. Jib and his ten friends, which
made eleven, joining our intimate evening.

The men all worked in banking or on Wall Street
and only wanted to discuss money, or what they'd
bought or would buy with theirs, while the women
were agents or models who laughed politely and added
sparkle to the conversation. These were the sort of
people who held real jobs which took them to exotic
places where people would listen to what they said.
They earned free tickets from frequent flying, worked
out at a gym with a trainer, balanced their checkbooks,
kept their many appointments, knew where to have
their hair cut and how to use mousse. I laughed when
everyone else did, sipped my wine, and checked and
rechecked my watch. When the Sambucas arrived
Blase casually sauntered over to Jib, whispered something, and they pretended to shake hands. I could see
the edge of the little envelope sticking out of Blase's
fist as he headed for the men's. Then Jib was seated
beside me, looking right at me, maybe for the first time
ever. "You know, we've never really had a chance to
talk," he said and smiled. "Now what is it you do
again?"

After Blase had finally paid the check and we were

standing on the street with Jib and his friends, waving at cabs, Blase sniffled, pinched his nostrils, then said, "We're heading off to R.T. It opened last week and it's supposed to be great, like an old mansion inside with sitting rooms and fireplaces and waitresses dressed like French maids—"

"Why don't we go home?" I said and pinched his bottom.

"I wouldn't mind a good night's sleep for a change, but I already told Jib I'd go," Blase said, as if being true to his word were a principle of his.

"We could read something brilliant and amusing," I said. "Like Wodehouse or Waugh."

"Darling, when I feel like reading something brilliant and amusing I just sit down and write," he replied. "But you do look tired."

Another night alone in bed.

The following Saturday I woke early, at Blase's prodding, and dragged myself across town to a bland-looking building with tiny windows, like a hospital. In the lobby was a cheery sign in pink and blue and yellow informing the aesthetically ignorant of the location of "Days of the Week Beauty Seminar." *Seminar*—the first I'd attended since "Indexicality, Rigid Designators, and the Possible Worlds Semantics of David Lewis." This time I didn't bring a notebook.

The seminar room looked like the dressing room for the Rockettes. For our $750 fee, we each had temporary use of a desk with a round mirror circled by a polka dot of bulbs. On each desk—there must have been fifty of them—was a name tag already filled in, and a pencil box color-coded for our day of the week. I was a Wednesday. The box contained a tube of mascara, three blushes, four eye shadows, powder, two eye pencils (everyone got black and brown), two vials of foundation, a brown lip pencil (which said "Neutral" on the bottom), three lipsticks, and three brushes—but they were all tiny, like a child's version of the real thing.

A woman with a very white face and matching hair pulled so tightly on top of her head you couldn't tell where skin ended and hair began—so I actually thought she was bald when I first entered the room—began distributing handouts to the women assembled. There were Helpful Hints for eyes, lips, cheeks, the whole face, and one that said "Danger Zones" across the top with a skull and crossbones underneath. We were instructed to wash our faces, then tone, then moisturize. Along the wall were two enormous scullery sinks like troughs, and all the days of the week began shoving and elbowing their way toward them, then splashing water, toner, and moisturizer all over themselves and the floor. Once clean, toned, and moist, we took our seats.

"Ladies?" the woman said. Her mouth was bright red, like fresh blood in snow. "Ladies? Shall we begin?"

She explained that the handouts would be discussed later; first, we were going to learn the Basics of our Art.

"You all have your day before you," she said, which was supposed to be amusing, I guess, since it was nine A.M., and some Fridays chuckled.

"Now let us begin to create a Beautiful You. Think of a painter," she began. "A painter at his blank canvas. By the end of this session, you will *all* be artists." She fell silent for a moment, allowing us to feel the full effect of this exciting news.

"First," she resumed, "the canvas must be gessoed." Then by way of translation she began to slop foundation on her face. "Like so," she said. "Four dabs on the cheeks, one on the chin, three on the forehead, and one on the nose. Go ahead now, ladies, dab." She kept us dabbing by relentlessly intoning, "Dab, dab. Dab, dab."

Next we were going to learn the Challenge of Blending. "With your fingertips, gently, like this," and she started smearing the stuff around on her face. *"Gently!"* she cautioned an overanxious student in the front row.

"Now what does the artist do next?" No one said anything. "He takes his brush and begins to apply his medium of self-expression," she revealed, taking up her white-handled brush and beginning to stroke on a bright red blush.

"You mean his *paint*," offered a smart-ass Saturday sitting in the back, of course.

"We prefer to call it your *medium of self-expression*," she said, reproachfully. "Now, stroke, stroke, stroke—and don't forget to blend!"

Lots of stroking and blending.

"Excuse me, ma'am?" A blond woman had her hand in the air. "But my medium of self-expression is all dried up."

"Well, just spit in it," the woman said.

To hell with Art. I went across the street and found a pay phone.

"A dozen red roses," I said. "And I want the card signed with a heart, that's all."

"Nothing else? Just 'with a heart'?" the woman said.

"Not the *words*. Just draw a heart."

I looked in shop windows, threw coins in the Plaza fountain, and stopped on Third for a cup of coffee, but I still reached our place before the flowers. Blase wasn't up, so I made a lot of noise, turned on the stereo, ground coffee beans, to try to rouse him. But the doorbell rang and the delivery woman handed me the bouquet and left and Blase still hadn't come down. I stuck the flowers in a vase, propped the card between two roses, and went upstairs. Blase lay motionless in bed. I opened the curtains. No movement. I pulled the vacuum from the closet and turned it on.

"Huh? What?" Blase sat up.

I switched off the vacuum. "Oh, sorry. I didn't see you here. I figured you'd gone out."

"What time is it?"

"Eleven forty-two."

"Shit! I'm s'posed to meet Andrea at noon."

"Who's Andrea?"

"Italian journalist."

Blase dressed, brushed his teeth, and ran downstairs.

As he searched for his wallet, I said, "Blase. Look at these," and gestured toward the flowers.

"Nice," he said, and pulled the door behind him.

Later he asked me, "Where'd these come from?"

"I don't know," I said. "Someone sent them."

"Man, there's nothing my fans won't do."

"They were for *me*," I said.

Blase raised his eyebrows. "How 'bout that. They're trying to reach me through you." With a jolt, he checked his Rolex. "Hey—if you're going to fix yourself up, you'd better start now. We're supposed to be at Steinberg's at eight."

That night we were going to a cocktail party at the home of a wealthy magazine publisher. Blase chose my outfit, then told me to apply my makeup as I'd been taught that day. I smeared on lipstick and a little mascara, returned to the bathroom and stroked on blush and eye shadow after Blase complained that I still looked "too plain Jane."

"How's this?"

"Not purple," Blase said.

"Huh?"

"On the lids. Not purple. Try brown."

An hour later I'd passed inspection and we were cabbing up and over to Seventy-first and Park. "Don't worry, I'll tell you who's who," Blase said.

At the door of the apartment, we were greeted by the magazine publisher himself, who resembled the L.A. Lakers' coach with his too-tight suit and his smarmy good looks. The publisher had an entourage of almost-beautiful agents and editors and publishers who all introduced themselves to Blase and said what a delight it was to meet him and how much they'd loved his book, and then they gave me a little nod and I nodded back.

We were ushered into an enormous room with masterpieces on the walls, fine Oriental carpets on the floors, and on the carpets, the well- and badly heeled shoes of writers and editors and a few editorial assistants who'd made lucky guesses about just whom to sleep with—at least, this was the kind of stuff Blase was whispering to me. While Blase was securing drinks, a woman with a classic twenties bob and body began chatting with me about the latest Broadway hit—then all of sudden, Blase grabbed my elbow and excused us and pulled me to the center of the room. "Don't bother with her," he said. "She's only a reader at W.D." He handed me my drink and while taking a sip from his he cast his gaze about the room. *"There,"* he said. "If you want to talk with a stranger, go charm him," and he nodded toward a medium-height, medium-build, medium-brown-haired man sipping from a martini glass by the piano. "He's the book editor at the *Daily*." Blase gave me a little push on the back toward the man. I turned and saw Blase hurrying off to talk with a fortyish woman with grey hair and a thin, pruney face wearing a velour jumpsuit.

Later, while I was admiring a Matisse by the window, Blase slid his arm around my waist and said, "So what'd you say to Michael Burton?"

"Who?"

"The book editor."

"Oh. I told him he reviews too much fiction."

Blase coughed into his drink. "What?"

"I told him that it was something of a crime failing to review Dennett's book on free will," I continued. "And then I told him that he should *never* allow deconstructionists to review philosophy books, like—"

"You said all that?" Blase looked horrified.

"Yeah."

"Did he know you're my wife?"

"Yeah."

Blase stepped on my foot. "I can't take you anywhere," he said.

Suddenly a shadowy figure appeared behind Blase, a huge dark arm fell over his shoulder.

"Isn't this sweet?" Jib said. "Young geezers in love."

Jib and Blase exchanged bits of party gossip, then Jib said, "Come with me, O ye blind and faithless. I am Plato, and I shall lead you out of the cave of ignorance and banality and into the light of the Beautiful, the Good, the True, and the Fun."

We followed Jib into a small room, empty except for two chairs, a desk, and a phone. Jib tapped a pile of coke from a small brown vial onto the desk and chopped it. We did the lines, and Jib said, "Anyone for seconds?" As he chopped more lines, Blase scooted off to get more drinks.

By the time we were finishing fourths, Blase was on the phone looking to secure more, and Jib was saying things to him like, "Tell him he *owes* me," and my head was reeling. I vaguely remember putting my hand on Jib's shoulder to steady myself; then I was in Jib's arms. Jib's fat lips were on mine. I was leaning way back. I could hear Blase laughing. I felt like my head would touch the floor. Fat lips on mine. Hayek. Hayek. "Bingo!" *Snap*.

Blase kept saying, "*Now* we're having fun." He meant all the attention and money and limos and drugs and glamorous new friends, I suppose, but with all this fun, I found myself sleeping late and waking hungover and some days phoning in to cancel class. One afternoon I decided to call the chairman of the philosophy department and explain that the facts of my life were no longer consistent with my teaching. I was thirty now, my husband needed me, I'd have to leave, but when I finally got him on the phone, the chairman simply said, "Roberts will be taking over your classes next week. And we won't be renewing your teaching appointment for fall." I wasn't surprised. I wasn't relieved. I was hungover still so I was a bit numb. Later, I comforted myself with the thought that I could still finish the thesis. I'd work on my own. I'd take my time.

We hadn't seen David or Claire for weeks. I'd lost ten pounds and people began asking Blase if I was ill. I'd stopped menstruating regularly so the odds of sparking a new life seemed dim. Besides, all this fun made it impossible for Blase to get it up.

Having fun entails a lot of sacrifices.

A year and a half after the publication of *Dark Night*, Blase decided we needed a bigger place so we could have even more fun, and two months later we moved into a roomy apartment on Sutton Place with two bedrooms, three and a half baths, a study, a cozy den, a full dining room, and off the living room, a thirty-foot patio with an electric canopy. Blase said it had to be furnished in Memphis and Modern Italian, and that meant overstuffed leather couches and chairs, tall thin lamps that bent like storks, pillars and walls of mirrors and strange sculptures and in the bedroom, grey and blue and pale green. "But I like English country," I said, and Blase promised that when we bought our summer house in Westport, I could do it however I wanted.

Now that I didn't have a job, and since Blase did lunch most days until cocktails, then did cocktails until dinner, then did dinner until party time when he came home and dressed me and put me on his arm and strutted out into the night, I spent a lot of time alone, and I guess I was having so much fun it didn't even feel like fun. The apartment was large, and I was small and getting smaller.

One morning I was sitting on the grey leather love seat with a cup of coffee and a hangover, watching Blase sitting on a grey leather love seat with a cup of coffee and a hangover, talking about himself with a frosted brunette in a fuzzy pink sweater. But over three and a half million Americans were watching Blase through the window of their TVs, and only one—our new cleaning woman, Zara—was watching me. Blase was charming ("Love your sweater") and articulate (except for a smattering of "uhs" and "likes" and "you knows" gluing together a few thoughts), though he did manage to rock in and out of the scope of the camera a number of times.

At six o'clock that morning, Blase, who'd brought us home at five o'clock, called to me from his bathroom, "Is my car here yet?" I looked out the window, down into the street, and saw a shiny black limo as long as our block and said, "I guess so." Funny how the changes in our life had changed the meanings of so many words: "car" now meant limo. "Powder" meant cocaine. "We'll have fun" meant I'd stand off at the side of the room and watch Blase regale a crowd of strangers. "I'll be home early" meant "Don't wait up."

I watched from the window as a blond woman in a skintight tuxedo opened his door. Blase said something that made the blond toss her hair and laugh. Then she closed Blase's door, got in the limo, and they drove off to the studio.

Blase was now thanking all the people who had helped him along the way: his parents, of course, and Jib, and Cam Warner, and David, and a maître d' or two, and three club owners, and two women whose names I didn't recognize. I waited. "And I especially want to thank my wife, my helpmeet, my first reader, the joy of my heart—Toby." But it didn't come. He'd finished the thanking and the woman smiled a toothful smile and thanked him and he thanked her and the studio living room was replaced by a bathroom in which a man was washing his hands with a special kind of soap that was guaranteed to get the crud out. I thought I'd like to wash Blase's mouth with that.

* * *

The more *Dark Night* sold, the more interviews that appeared; the more interviews that appeared, the more invitations that came flooding in, and Blase was hard-pressed to turn anything down.

"It's my research," he said. "Now that the *Daily* wants me to write the 'In and Out' column, I need to be out there observing the trends."

This was not true. What was true was that I would read the New York gossip magazines and write comments in the margins; then Blase would take up the magazines and scribble notes from what I'd written. No sooner had I observed that cumberbunds were never going to appear beneath suits as *Datum* had claimed than I'd read it in Blase's column. And little stories I'd relate to him about things that happened to me—like the one about the man who came up to me at Rockefeller Center while I was watching the skaters, kissed me, stepped back, and said, "Oh, sorry"—would appear a few days later, stretched out and embellished, as things that had happened to him.

"How could I possibly determine what's In and what's Not In from my living room couch? Besides," Blase added, "you know I get my ideas for fiction from real life. I have to *live*, Toby."

Blase endorsed products: a cognac, a kind of snazzy new sunglasses, and even men's bikini underwear. We went to the most popular restaurants where Blase insisted on the most public tables and then complained about his new lack of privacy when people noticed him. Taxicabs were for the rubes, Blase said, so we only rode in *cars*. Blase checked the gossip columns each day for references to him, his clothes, his movements around the city, which they faithfully reported.

"You're making a fool of yourself," I said.

"It's the media, Bunny," Blase said. "They want me to *be* the character from *Dark Night* so they buy me drinks and take me to clubs and make me pose with women. Do you think *I* like it? It's not my choice."

"Look what they're saying about you—that you're not a serious writer, that you're a partyer and a playboy."

"Honestly, I don't care what they're saying about me as long as they're talking," he said.

"Don't you want to be taken seriously?"

"Of course I do," Blase said. "Look, they said all this about Fitzgerald, too."

"But that was *Fitzgerald*," I wanted to say. Instead I said, "And look what happened to him." More than once Blase had told me the pathetic story of Scott and Zelda until finally I sat down and read Turnbull and Mizener and Milford. Theirs was a story of excess and vanity. Waste.

I suppose I must have looked terribly worried because Blase took my hand and looked into my eyes and said, "This must be very hard for you, Bunny. I know I cast a long shadow." But that wasn't what I'd meant at all.

As more interviews began to appear in newspapers and magazines across the country, I noticed that Blase never mentioned the fact that he was married, though one reporter revealed that "he currently lives in New

York City with a relative." At cocktail parties, dinner parties, and clubs, Blase would introduce me simply as Toby and some people would say to him, "I didn't know you had a sister" or to me, "I heard you were a paraplegic!"

When it came out that Blase really was married, nobody seemed to care.

"Why should they?" Claire said. We had met for tea at the Plaza. We were in the Palm Court drinking beer and eating petit fours and tea cakes. "It's not the fifties, Toby. Being married these days is just another temporary fact about someone, like their address. Let's put it this way: it's never stopped me."

Two months earlier, a woman from a national magazine had phoned to tell us we'd been chosen one of the ten most beautiful couples in America. Would we accept the honor and kindly come to Doodles photo studio the following week?

I had said, "Thanks anyway," but Blase phoned her back and said, "Of course."

At the studio we were photographed kissing, hugging, holding hands. On breaks they fed us caviar and filled our glasses with champagne. The photo that finally appeared in the magazine was of me looking desperately at Blase, Blase smiling broadly into the camera.

"When we did this couples photograph, I thought women would think, 'Shucks, he's taken,' and respect that. But shit, Claire, they still elbow me out of the way and fawn all over him like he's up for grabs."

"And he lets them," she said.

* * *

That evening Isabelle called. She'd seen the magazine at the dentist's office. "Are you sure you're okay?"

"Fine," I said. "Just waking up from a nap." Though I was rather drunk and having some trouble figuring out which end of the receiver to speak in, I saw no need to mention it, since she hadn't asked.

"In this picture, I mean," she said, "you look so—*sad*."

"I was tired," I said.

"But your eyes look so glassy, like you're about to cry."

"I had a cold," I said.

"But you're okay now?"

"Of course," I said. "Sure. Fine." It was amazing how easily the lies came when what you were lying about was alcohol or drugs.

Blase was waving from the door of the bedroom.

"Gotta fly," I said and hung up.

"Fly is right," Blase said. "You ready?"

I was sitting on the bed in my bathrobe. "My hair," I said.

"Looks fine," he said. He grabbed a black dress from the closet. "Wear this."

While I was stroking mascara on my lashes, trying not to poke my eyeball, music suddenly filled the apartment. Blase had had speakers installed in every room, including the bathrooms, and now a frantic conga-powered tune drowned out the thoughts that had been struggling for shape in my head. Doing a little cha-cha with shoulder rolls, Blase danced into the bathroom carrying a tray covered with long fat worms of cocaine.

"Strengthening powders for Madame."

Leaning over the tray with the bill up my nose, I saw that the tray was only newly a tray—formerly it was a framed eight-by-ten wedding photograph of Blase and me. When I sniffed a line, a tear fell onto the glass and the powder covering Blase's image disappeared.

"You okay?"

"Sure. Just got some mascara in my eye," I said.

Blase laughed and licked the puddle from the glass.

"Briny," he said.

The buzzer went off.

"Must be Jib. Man's got an uncanny sense of timing." Blase set the photograph on the vanity. "You get it," he added, lowering his face to the glass.

"Glad to see you're rich in supplies," Jib said. Blase was turning a few tablespoons of cocaine into a few lines the length and width of filterless Camels. We were in a room with breathtaking views of the city, fine art on the walls, sitting around the coffee table, all our attention focused on the substance on the glass. "However, I brought provisions, just in case."

"Toby, our friend here looks weary from his long journey uptown. Why don't you make him one of your strengthening cocktails? Actually, though I'm feeling my usual robust self, I'll take one too, as a prophylactic." He shot a look at Jib. "While you're at it, why don't you make one for yourself, darling. You're looking rather drawn."

As I filled three glasses with frozen vodka, I felt myself growing tight and breathless. Too fast. I felt as

I imagined one must feel when on the brink of a panic or heart attack except that every synapse in my brain sparked with the news that I was on the verge of something great. Power. Strength. Insight. One more line and I could do anything. Then I heard Blase snap his fingers, even above the music and the loud quick beat of my heart.

The thumping of the bass, the back beat powering the dancers on the floor way below, aligned itself with the tempo of my breathing and finally became a tapping on my arm.

" 'Scuse me."

A woman. To the side of my body with the hand I didn't write with was a woman talking to me with enormous pale lips lined in black. The lipstick was shiny and light but so thick I couldn't tell whether it spread beyond normal lips making them appear smooth and puffed or whether it marked off a real mouth. The woman spoke for a while so I watched carefully to see how the skin would move with bilabials and fricatives. The alleged lips puckered and smacked and finally separated and stayed separated exposing teeth that overlapped on top. I looked up and noticed the woman was staring at me. Oh. She was smiling. She leaned close.

"Did ja hear me?" she said.

"No." I had to say it loud.

"I asked whether you're Blase Regenhere's date tonight." The woman was yelling in my ear. Her hair was in my face.

"His *date*? Is that what you said? Am I his *date*," I yelled in her hair.

"Yeah," she yelled back.

"Hell no," I said. I laughed. I tasted hair spray.

"Great," she said, and she kissed my cheek and then she was gone.

It seemed I was in Bloomingdale's, it was so dark and the lights were so small and glittery, but we were in a nightclub somewhere on the Lower East Side. An old Loew's theater. Shadowy figures moved behind me, here, on the mezzanine.

"Blase?"

No one replied.

The music was pounding with my heart— *"No dust, no dust, no dust"*—someone sliding their hand around my waist—*"It's over, it's over"*—it lets go.

"Cigarette?"

A man in darkness stands with a flame.

"Blase?"

He holds the light to his face. A startled face because, I realize, it has no eyebrows.

How long have I been here on this mezzanine?

I remember: outside the club, flashbulbs and Blase's hand planted in the small of my back, hurrying me up a staircase, down a dark hall, up another staircase and into a small room with a bar. Skinny blond women with large breasts. Tanned men with long wavy hair and shirts opened under their tuxedos. Blase and Jib know everyone. I'm pulled from Blase's arm and shoved out of the way, back through the crowd, lost in an undertow of strangers. From far away I watch as Blase holds forth for his fans, hayekking, snapping. I sit on a couch of leather cushions in primary colors, small round cushions that don't touch, like a row of piano stools welded together. Someone kisses the top of my head. Someone takes my hand and licks it and I am crying. Then weight on my shoulders.

"Hey, Toby. It's Jib."

I want it to be Blase. I wish it so completely I say, "Blase?"

"No, it's Jib."

"I need to go," I say.

"You need refreshments."

I look him full in the face. "Really. Good God, Jib, I'm *dying*."

Jib pushes me back against the wall. Then it's Jib's voice, "Yo, Blase," "Hey, get Blase," "Where the fuck is Regenhere," and "Tell him his wife's dying."

I run from the room and climb down stairs and hurry along dark hallways and walk up ramps until I'm a shadow among these shadows. And I hear someone say: *"No one here can see you"* and *"A place where I can be alone"* and I listen closely until someone taps my arm.

And now, the same voice sings of fantastic dreams spawning false hopes becoming fatal expectations; weak minds stumbling on a thought and breaking; weak hearts skipping beats, never mending; love and honor in a time outworn; death, and betrayal from the inside; courage, redemption, and home.

Then I was sitting outside the club leaning against the building, just inside the space marked off by the velvet cord, waiting for Blase. The ponytailed bouncer said it was okay, I could sit there if I really wanted. I thanked him and he yawned.

"There's a metal ball on your tongue," I said.

"Got it last summer. Like it?" The bouncer stuck out his tongue and wagged it, making the ball wiggle.

"How does it stay there?" I asked.

"It's *pierced*," he said, like I was an idiot on drugs, which I was.

The crowd beyond the velvet cord was so still, their activities so hushed, as if they were posing for a mural or waiting in the wings for their cues, and this calmed the commotion in my head.

I'd stopped checking the faces of the departing when finally I heard Blase's voice: "*There* you are. Christ, Toby, I've been looking everywhere for you. Everyone's going to Suzanne's for her version of group therapy. Hey, what are you doing down there?" He helped me up.

The door to the club opened and Jib breezed out.

"Oh man!" he said, slapping Blase's back. "I'm in *love*."

Blase laughed. "With that bimbo in the gold shoes?"

The bouncer unhooked the cord and we moved onto the sidewalk.

"That was no ordinary bimbo. Woman starred at Exeter and Yale—now she's the enfant terrible of Goldman Sax."

"Ah, one of that rare species," Blase said. "The highly prized bimbo savant."

*　*　*

Blase finally brought us home at five-thirty, wired and restless and raw. We lay in bed, staring at the early morning news and drinking vodka, not talking. After a while Blase began to snore, but my eyes wouldn't stay closed. I was trembling and the bedclothes wouldn't warm me. I put my arms around Blase, threw my legs over his. The prospect of eventually falling asleep was thin comfort because I knew I'd simply wake, hungover, and after a few hours' recovery, just when the world would start to come in focus, the whole thing would begin again. Then I saw my life as a series of wasted nights and desperate mornings like this, and I realized it could go on this way, repeating itself into my future until I died or killed myself.

I dressed and walked over to the river.

For a while I looked out across the water, waiting for the sun to rise, watching the sky turn from black to charcoal to grey. *The moment of my death is the end of my world,* I thought, *a precise moment when nothing will be anything to me waiting in the future.* Why was this terrifying? There was a moment before which I was nothing to the world and the world was nothing to me and this fact I regarded with indifference. But somehow it felt unbearable that there should be a similar time in the future.

Then it struck me: Should I continue leading my life as I now led it, swinging between hungover and drunk all the way up until the moment of demise, I would have been the kind of person about whom a few people—my parents, my sisters, Claire—might say, "She could have been someone" and they would be full of regret because they would have painfully, impotently witnessed a life poorly lived.

I remembered Nietzsche: Live your life as if you were creating a work of art; put those things you find most beautiful in it. Something like that.

When Blase had finished the quart of chocolate milk I'd picked up on my way back to the apartment, I told him about my decision.

"You're not even going to drink?"

"No."

"Never?"

"At least for now."

Blase smiled and nodded, but then seemed genuinely surprised when I stayed home that night, and the next, and the next.

"You're serious about this?"

"Yeah."

Though I tried, I couldn't ever seem to talk Blase into staying home, even when I wore spiked heels, a Charo wig, and peekaboo lingerie.

Some mornings I'd wake to find Jib and Blase crashed out on the couches in the living room, snoring loudly, an empty bottle of Jack Daniels and a finger-smeared mirror on the coffee table between them. I still hurried out to the corner store to get chocolate milk for Blase's hangover. It was one of the tiny threads holding me in place as his wife. But mostly I woke alone.

Sometimes it seemed to me that there was an infinite number of Blases—possible Blases—one for each different turn his life might have taken. I could see them standing to one side of him, as if they radiated from him, ordered in terms of their similarity to him. The closest ones were almost halos around the flesh-and-blood Blase, Blase with minor changes: shorter hair, cleaner nails, a different suit on. It was as if Blase was somehow not really himself, he was one of these other Blases—one that didn't stay out all night and do cocaine—and I could see him stepping into that Blase like feet into old shoes.

"What are you looking for out there?"

Blase and Jib and I were sitting in the den, watching the late news. I guess they wanted to be up-to-date before they went back out into the Danger Zone.

Jib smiled. "Me, I look for lonely fourteen-year-old bimbos, turn 'em on to some blow, fuck their brains out in the ladies', then drown 'em in the toilet. A dirty job, but someone's gotta do it." He was laughing. "Scotty here, he's a bit of prude—he'll only fuck 'em in the men's." Blase hayekked.

Like little boys playing G.I. Joe—"You be Kennedy and I'll be Khrushchev"—at some point Jib began calling Blase "Scott" and Blase began calling Jib "Ernie" or "Papa" as if they'd decided to be Hemingway and Fitzgerald, which, apparently, they had. They liked appearing together in public, since then there would be lots of write-ups in the columns, since Jib's book had come out and it was scandalous too, and so created its own sensation. They were now the two hottest young writers in New York and they thought "hottest" meant best and "New York" meant the world.

Before they left, I pulled Blase aside. "When will you be home?"

"When the fun runs out."

"How do you think it makes me feel," I asked, "when you and Jib leave at eleven and don't return until ten, noon, whatever, the next day? I *worry* about you, Blase."

"Don't worry," Blase said. "And I won't be home late." Sure enough, when I woke the next morning there they were, Jib and Blase, sitting at the dining room table, passing a bottle of Jack Daniels back and forth, snorting lines. Two young women were seated with them. One had brown hair to her waist; the other's head was covered with curling flames of red. Both were dressed in slinky black and pearls.

"I got home at *four*," Blase said, proudly, "so you wouldn't worry." This was supposed to make me happy.

"He *did*!" said the woman seated to his right, the redhead, almost in his lap.

"Join us," Blase said, and I sat down. I was wrapped in a terry robe, no makeup, like the boring old mom you meet at the end of prom night.

The brunette leaned over and touched the back of my hand. "We were just saying that today's Marty's birthday," she said, gesturing at the redhead.

"Happy birthday," I said.

Blase was chopping at a pile of powder, sliding his jaw side-to-side; drops of sweat slid down his grey face.

217

The brunette continued: "Then we found out it's Jib's birthday in two weeks and Blase just had his and mine's the nineteenth! We're all Leos!" Except me of course: I was a Cancer.

The two young women nodded together, agreed that Leos were cool, while Jib offered me a line.

"No thanks."

"Why didn't you come out tonight, Toby?" the redhead, Marty, said.

"I was busy," I said, and Blase smiled.

The brunette rose, skipped over to the stereo, and began looking through our tapes. "Got any Black Uhuru?" she said.

Everything ran out around noon and the young women finally left. Blase and Jib kissed them good-bye, like good friends. I dressed and left for the library while Blase and Jib hunted for more liquor.

The librarian read the spine. "*Ecce Homo.* The words with which Pilate presented Christ to his accusers, if memory serves." I was impressed—"By Friedrich . . . Nit-ski"—briefly.

I flipped to the table of contents: "Why I Am So Wise," "Why I Am So Clever," "Why I Write Such Good Books." Sounded like stuff Blase could've penned. Maybe it was time to go back to Aristotle.

Blase was suddenly sort of famous, suddenly sort of rich, suddenly sort of hip, and all of this certainly answered his fondest childhood dream. Long before this, when we were first together, Blase had told me he was a shy boy, slight and bookish, and the other kids, the cool kids, the kids on the inside, never included him in their naughtiness, but made him a victim of it. Blase tried to elbow his way in by becoming a disciplinary case—setting off fire alarms, putting tacks on teachers' chairs, starting food fights in the cafeteria—but as in chess, the frontal attack rarely works. There was a time when Blase's catching on to a trend—Beatles boots, hip-huggers, yo-yos—meant the trend was over. But now he'd made it: the cool kids were now cool adults and they all liked him, looked to him to define what was hip and what wasn't. All his life he'd dreamed of occupying this position and he wasn't going to abdicate without a promise of something better. Funny, he had told me this story of being on the outside looking in as if it weren't the story of every child, as if it explained something unique about him.

The problem for me was finding the lure out of this life, something Blase would be able to recognize as lasting and valuable, more valuable than hobnobbing with models, actors, and artists, more valuable than doing drugs, riding in limos, and setting trends, more valuable than being the temporary spokesman of this generation. Having a family wasn't better—it was boring. Dirty diapers and square meals and family vacations were the antithesis of cool and chic. The only solution I could think of was getting Blase out of New York. That was the *real* problem: the city, with its clubs and drugs and shallow people and glittery parties. In his heart of hearts Blase was serious, deeply sensitive, artistic. He needed to be reminded of his most profound dreams and his deepest values. Then he would recall that house by the sea with meadows and gardens and wooded glens and shaggy dogs and children. A reflective, serene life was what he'd always wanted.

"You want to go to law school in *Maine*?" Blase said.

"Portland," I said. "It's a good, small law school."

"There are lots of good law schools around here."

"But I think it would be a nice time to buy our house, what with interest rates being so low and all," I said.

"But what would *I* do in Maine?"

"Write, for one," I said. "You are a *writer*, no?"

"What would I write about? Compost? Dandelions? Leaky pipes?"

"How 'bout people?" I said.

"Bunny, I'm a New York writer."

"You don't have to be here to write about New York, do you? Isn't imagination the wellspring of fiction?"

"I'm a sponge," he said. "I absorb what's around me. That's what I write about. You can't expect me to suddenly change because you've decided you don't like the city."

"It's not that," I said. "It's just that, well, I thought the country would be a better place for our baby."

"Yeah, I'm sure it would be."

I smiled.

Blase stared at me.

I didn't say anything.

Then he blinked, took in a quick breath and said, "Oh my God. Are you pregnant?"

Don't do it, I thought, but I kept smiling.

"I guess once *is* enough." He looked at his feet, brought his hand to his forehead. "Christ!"

Stop it now, I thought.

Blase grabbed me by the shoulders. He began shaking his head. "No, Toby. God, no. This is the *wrong* time."

The man was panicked. The man was desperate. But I couldn't say anything.

"Toby," he said. "Darling," he said. He was still shaking his head. "Not *now*."

He glanced at his feet, shook his head some more. "No."

Then he squeezed my arms tightly, looked at my eyes. "Tell me it's not true, Bunny. Tell me you're joking."

"It's not true," I said. "I'm joking," I said.

I decided to take the LSAT in September and wrote to the Law School Admissions Services for the registration packet. I rooted through my old files and found a short story I still liked, sent it to a women's magazine. I collected my "Animal Apparel" cartoons, did some editing, added color, and submitted them to a publishing house. But when the rejection for the short story arrived, I collected all my work and shoved it in the back of the hall closet. Maybe I'd ace the LSAT.

One morning I woke and found myself alone in the apartment. No message from Blase on the answering machine. I put on a pot of coffee and began to look around, shuffled into Blase's study and sat at his desk. I suddenly noticed the living urn plant on the window: the flower had lost all its color and the leaves were sagging and grey. The two babies were yellow and suffering too.

I collected all the little toys Blase had bought, the toys he once needed to fill the space between inspirations, to keep a rhythm and motion alive while his thoughts momentarily idled. Since he'd begun his career, I hadn't heard these toys or the sporadic click of keys on the computer. Blase explained that he didn't have time to write now that he was engaged in the important business of establishing himself as a literary figure. I wound up all the toys.

Whiz-bang. Clatter-clang. Ding-ding.

I opened one of the drawers of the desk.

A pile of unanswered correspondence.

Postcards.

A photograph of us from our wedding.

And at the back of the drawer, buried beneath elastic bands and a box of paper clips and an old checkbook, a long white business envelope, something addressed to Blase and marked URGENT. PERSONAL AND CONFIDENTIAL.

It might as well have said, TOBY REGENHERE. OPEN IMMEDIATELY because I did.

NINE

Huis Clos

Here, then, was the note:

Dear Blase,

Since you won't meet with me, you've left me no choice but to write you, as ridiculous as that may seem, because I just can't let you go without having expressed my feelings.

You used to say everyone wanted you and Toby to be Scott and Zelda, so keeping up appearances was important on that score. But do you have any idea how much it hurt me to see you falling all over those girls at R.T.? Just what were you attempting to accomplish? If you wanted to anger me, you succeeded; if you wanted to pain me, you succeeded; but if you wanted to convince me that you're not gay, you did not succeed.

Look, I have no idea if you're "really" gay. That's for you to discover. All I know is that I trusted you and now I feel used, experimented on.

The letter closed with some words about a possible meeting and hopes that, in the future, Blase could be more careful with people's feelings. And the letter was signed:

Love,
JAMES HARTLEY

in capitals, just like that, first and last name, so I couldn't miss it, couldn't miss the fact that the wounded party was a *man, a man in love*. I read the letter again. I brewed another pot of coffee and read the letter again.

I phoned Claire, read her the letter.

"Jesus, Toby," she said. "What do you *think* it means?"

"This guy sounds like a jilted *lover*."

"Very good," Claire said.

"What do you think it could mean?" I said.

"Sounds like Blase is fucking a man."

"No," I said, holding out for the other interpretation.

"Yes he is," Claire said. "He's fucking this guy James Hartman."

"Hartley."

"Whatever."

"Blase likes women," I said.

"So? Don't be naive, Toby."

"I can't believe he'd be involved with a man."

"You've got the letter," Claire said.

"Yeah."

"I told you Blase would be Trouble," Claire said. "Maybe he's a *fag*."

"Yeah, well, then he's *my* fag." I considered. "No way. He's not gay. Not Blase." It would be one thing, one big fat difficult thing, to compete with a new woman when you're the same old woman, and I hadn't even been in training for *that*; how would I ever compete with a man?

"Toby." Claire sounded serious. "What about AIDS?" and everything was still.

In the front hall I paced, occasionally pausing to confront Blase in the mirror: "Well? What does this mean?" or "Who's James Hartley?" and, worst of all, "I want a divorce." But I didn't want a divorce. Blase was my husband, my friend, the best part of me, the only part of me with any substance; he was the love of my life; it's just that my life was nowhere right now. I'd failed him. Of course he went seeking satisfaction elsewhere—I wouldn't go out anymore. I wasn't any fun. I didn't even drink. I was a drag. But a *man*?

I faced the mirror again. "Blase, I need to know whether you're gay or bisexual or what. I mean, in this world of diseases—of AIDS . . . "

The door opened.

"What a night!"

"Blase!" I said, hugging him around the neck. I leaned back and looked at his face.

"Blase!" I yelled, slapping him hard.

"This will never come up as an issue in my life again," Blase said.

We were in the kitchen with five open boxes of Chinese. I wasn't eating.

"But what about *my* life?"

Blase took a gulp of wine.

"What about AIDS? How *could* you risk my life?" I slapped him again.

"I didn't," Blase said. "And would you please stop that? I'm trying to eat."

I threw my wine glass across the room. *"Answer me!"*

Blase took my hand and stroked it. "Calm down," he said. "You're really overreacting."

"Overreacting? Can you tell me how am I *supposed* to react, Blase, 'cause really I have no idea, I don't have a fucking clue—"

"Sit," Blase said, patting the kitchen table before my usual place. I braced myself against the doorframe. Blase poured himself another glass of wine. I was staring at him but he was looking at the glass or his hands. We were both breathing quickly. Then Blase pinched his nostrils, cleared his throat.

"I don't know what you think that note said that's making you so crazy." He took a sip of wine.

"Christ, Blase! Hartley said you were gay."

"No he didn't."

"Well he *implied* that you were."

"No he didn't"

"Okay, he said he didn't know whether you were *really* gay."

"Look, he *hopes* I'm gay, Toby."

"He said he felt used."

"He *wishes* I'd used him."

"Look Blase, it's obvious from the note that you had some sort of romantic encounter with Hartley."

"No it isn't and no I didn't."

"Where's the note?" I said.

Blase shrugged. "Beats me."

"Blase, the man is in love with you."

"Clearly," he said.

"And he feels you led him on."

"That's just wishful thinking on his part."

I pounded the doorframe with the side of my fist. "Blase! Are you trying to make me crazy 'cause if you're trying to make me crazy I'd really have to say I think you're succeeding 'cause right this minute I feel so goddammed crazy—"

"I don't know what you've imagined that note said, Toby, but you're getting hysterical."

"Well, you tell me what it said."

"Hartley just let me know he was pissed off and asked if I wanted to meet him sometime."

"I'm supposed to believe this?" Maybe it was what the note had said.

"Bunny, you'll just have to trust me," he said.

"Blase."

He rose from the table.

"*Please*, Blase."

He took a glass from the cupboard and filled it with wine.

"Here," he said, offering me the glass.

I stared at the glass in his hand. I took it and hurled it at the refrigerator. Glass flew, red wine streamed down the door of the refrigerator.

Blase's mouth was set flat and tight. Silently he turned back to the cupboard, removed another glass, and filled it.

"Here," he said again.

"God damn it!" I threw the glass. Wine ran down the front of the refrigerator, the base flew back at me.

Blase removed another glass from the cupboard. He emptied the bottle into the glass and held it out to me. I stared at his eyes. I wanted to dive into them and reclaim him, but they were hard and narrowed now.

"No," I said.

"Take it," he said.

I threw the glass but halfheartedly so it simply bounced off the refrigerator door, splattering wine everywhere but remaining whole.

The kitchen looked like the scene of an ax murder. Red everywhere. I turned away and began crying. Then Blase was rubbing my shoulders.

"Feel better?"

I couldn't speak.

"So we'll just drop it now, okay?"

But I couldn't drop it. I didn't know what Blase had done but then, I never knew what Blase did. I had no idea if he was really gay. All I kept thinking was, *this is too much. This is way too much.* From that night on, I slept in the guest room as if that might be punishment for Blase, which it wasn't because he hadn't slept with me for months anyway. He was either too loaded, not interested, not able, or not home.

During the next six weeks I wandered around Manhattan like a tourist. Things that had receded into the cityscape long before stepped out and became real for me again. I bought pretzels from street vendors, gave my change to strangers, rode the tramway, took and saved flyers thrust in my hands by representatives of innumerable lost causes, stood on the steps of the public library in awe, purchased three chapters of some woman's unpublished novel at a dollar a page. I wandered into shops and wrote checks for items that had no place in my life: an appointment book, a leather suitcase, bristol board, a layette set.

Occasionally I met David or Della or Claire for lunch or coffee.

"I don't think I can be in philosophy anymore," I said. "It's become so *painful*."

"Sounds like you need a new direction," David said.

"Yeah. I've been thinking about that."

"Any ideas?"

"I was thinking about maybe going to law school."

"God, you are desperate," he said.

"Toby, you need a *change*." We were at the Lion's Head. Della was sipping a coke.

"You're right," I said.

"Have you ever thought of confronting your most basic self? There's a colony in Hawaii set up precisely for that purpose. They start with the physical: they take away all your personal possessions—clothing, jewelry, anything you might use to objectify yourself—then they work on your character. They strip you of all your defenses until you're just a pure self. Then they completely rebuild you psychically."

"Sounds pretty radical."

"Of course some people think you can achieve

basically the same result with a handful of mushrooms. Or there's always primal scream therapy."

"I don't think so."

Della stared into her drink. "Have you considered dyeing your hair?"

"Toby?"

"Sorry I'm late." Though Claire insisted it was too bridge-and-tunnel, she'd finally agreed to meet me here at the Top of the Sixes.

"Your *hair*," she said.

"Yeah, I dyed it."

"It's *green*."

"It is?" I tried to make out my reflection in the window behind her. "It was supposed to be 'Lightest Late Summer Blond'."

"What'd you get?" She nodded at my shopping bag.

"Nothing."

"Come on," she said, as if I were holding out on her.

I slid the box from the bag.

"A mobile?"

"I thought it was cute," I said. "You know, clowns and moons and stars."

Claire didn't say anything.

"And primary colors are supposed to be good for developing early neuronal connections in infants," I said. "Plus it was on sale."

After we ordered, Claire coughed and took in a long breath and said, "Leave him."

"Who, Blase?"

"Yeah, Blase."

"But I love him."

"So?"

"You don't understand," I said. "We're not like other couples. We're best friends. We're partners. We're a *team*."

"Oh, Toby."

When Claire finally told me she thought maybe I should get some professional help, I grabbed my shopping bag and stormed out of the restaurant. *Some friend*, I thought.

When Claire phoned me that night I let the answering machine get it. She said she was sorry if she'd said anything to offend me. She said she was concerned about me. Over the next few weeks Isabelle, Kate, Anne, my mother, and Della all left messages on the answering machine too, but I never phoned them back. Things were too confusing right now. Nothing made sense right now. Everything was a mess right now. If I didn't understand it, how could they? Plus they'd never forgive Blase for betraying me, even if I could. I'd just wait and get in touch when things blew over, I thought, though I couldn't imagine how things could possibly blow over.

Soon our marriage seemed to be reduced to sneers and glares exchanged in the hall while Blase was on his way out or in, over coffee, or at the checkbook. Unlike most couples, however, we never argued, we never really *had* argued. I resolved one day that if we ever worked things out I would make sure to argue. Show me a couple who can't argue, I say, and I'll show you a couple of assholes.

I was outraged at the new Blase, waiting for the old Blase, the serious, loving, good Jekyll to resurface, indignant on my behalf, prepared to denounce his other self, a false self who never would have gotten a foothold in the world if it weren't for a certain curiosity and carelessness with dangerous potions.

One day Hollywood phoned. They loved Blase. They called him "babe." They wanted to meet him. Blase took the next plane and now he was staying at a posh hotel where famous people had died. He was given a car and a driver and a fat per diem. He was doing meals with all sorts of movie people, the behind-the-scenes people with unusual sexual appetites who had all the power and money. They were dining in bright restaurants with telephones on the tables. During his free time he was shopping on Rodeo Drive, dancing at glittery clubs. Meantime, I was wandering around my apartment by day listening to Bonnie Raitt and Patsy Cline sing about bad dreams and faded love, trying to plow through all of Poe by night.

The afternoon I spoke with Claire, I had been pacing the halls of our apartment to "Love Has No Pride," and in a daze induced by too much wine and premature nostalgia I answered the phone, forgetting I wasn't answering the phone anymore.

"Toby, are you okay?"

"Fine."

"Why haven't you returned my calls?" Claire asked.

"Sorry. I've been busy."

"Doing what?" Claire was pissed off.

"Why are you calling?"

"Have you seen Page Three?" Page Three was the *New York Mail's* gossip page, perhaps, on average, the most widely read words in New York City.

"No."

"Well, brace yourself. There's an item about Blase and some woman."

"What do you mean, 'some *woman*'?"

"Well, the name is Agnes and the vocation is 'starlet' so I'd guess we're talking woman here."

"And?" I said.

"The piece strongly suggests that she and Blase are an item," Claire said.

"Big deal," I said. "They make up stuff about Blase all the time."

"Yeah, maybe, but there's a photo," she said.

I threw a raincoat over my nightgown and got the paper from the corner grocery. The headline on Page Three said:

BLASE REGENHERE IS STEPPING OUT!

and underneath was a photograph of Blase and a woman, a skinny, sleazy-looking tramp, flat as Gumby, toothy as a horse, wrapped in Blase's arms outside the Plaza.

I'd seen this woman before, sneaking out of our

apartment with her shoes in one hand, a shopping bag in the other. Blase had explained that he'd been interviewing her for the position of secretary. "But I do all that work," I had said. He'd just wanted to take the pressure off me, to free me up, he'd said, so I might be able to spend my time more fruitfully. No one else ever applied for the alleged position and I forgot to ask him about the shoes.

A paragraph under the photo explained that Blase had been seen all over town in the company of starlet Agnes Airhead.

When I phoned him that night, read the item from Page Three, Blase said, "*That?* That was just business."

"Business? At the Plaza? Embracing?"

"Toby, she works for Illiteracy Inc. and she wants me to help organize a fund-raiser. That's all."

"Try again."

"Huh?"

"It's the same woman I saw *weeks ago* leaving our apartment. You said you were looking for a secretary. You said you were interviewing her."

"I did?"

I waited. I could hear the click and hum on the long distance line.

Then Blase blurted, "Okay—I love her. I do."

I hadn't expected that.

"You do?"

"Yes."

I started crying. "What about me?"

"I don't know. I just don't know."

* * *

Blase returned from Hollywood three days later. I met him at the airport. On the limo ride back to Manhattan I made him look me in the eyes while I recited this poem I'd memorized, from the book of Yeats he'd given me so long ago:

> "Though you are in your shining days,
>   Voices among the crowd
>   And new friends busy with your praise,
>   Be not unkind or proud,
>   But think about old friends the most:
>   Time's bitter flood will rise,
>   Your beauty perish and be lost
>   For all eyes but these eyes."

I was looking to pierce him right to his heart and re-claim it as mine.

Blase took my hands. He cleared his throat. "Toby," he began. "I want you to always remember this—me, so famous, coming back from Hollywood, where I was flown first-class, given my own car and driver, a monstrous expense account. Us, in this limo on this sunny afternoon, you reciting this poem to me"—my heart was beating wildly, here it comes, I thought—"so one day you can tell my biographer."

I'm sure my mouth fell open. I'm sure my eyes bugged. *My heart is broken*, I thought. But then the sound I heard wasn't my sobbing, or my open palm slapping his face. I was *laughing*. I was cracking up.

"What," Blase said.

I was laughing so hard I thought I'd lift off the seat.

Blase started smiling. He said, "What? What?" which made me laugh even more deeply, so I couldn't catch my breath, so my stomach muscles were aching. It was so damn funny. *So you can tell my biographer!*

Blase began to laugh too, which made me laugh harder. And he kept saying it: "What? What? What's so funny?"

The next week we were in the office of a marriage counselor Blase had surprised me by agreeing to see. We were seated in stuffed chairs across a wide desk from the counselor.

I began. I looked at Blase. I explained about the note from James Hartley.

"Toby thinks a marriage is like a bone," Blase responded. He was staring at the counselor.

I explained about Agnes.

"She thinks it can break and then heal, and maybe even be stronger than it was at the start."

I brought up cocaine, alcohol.

"But I think a marriage is more like meat. Once it spoils it's garbage—and there's only one thing you can do with garbage."

I began to cry. *Garbage?*

TEN

The End, Revisited

Preparing oneself for pain doesn't make it hurt less—just ask any experienced student of Lamaze. It's like preparing for death when you're not suicidal: you don't want it to come, no matter how braced your self is—except if you're some religious or spiritual fanatic for whom the end is not really the end.

The morning after our session with the marriage counselor Blase woke me up. "I'm leaving," he said. Then he turned and calmly walked away.

I ran out to the front hall.

The door was open. Blase was adjusting the collar of his raincoat in the mirror.

"What?"

"I'm leaving."

"Don't leave!" I screamed it. I grabbed his arm. I fell to my knees.

"I'm not in love with you. There's nothing to continue this marriage for. I love Agnes. Good-bye." He slammed the door behind him.

My apartment, our apartment: smelling of cleaning fluids and citrus, just the same, I supposed, as it had been moments before when Blase was still here, when it still seemed there was a chance. Into the living room and it felt like I'd caught everything off guard, like all had been in motion before I walked in. I found myself snooping, going through Blase's drawers, his jacket pockets, his jewelry case, looking for and finding clues to what he'd been up to these past few weeks or months. Love notes from Agnes quoting rock-and-roll lyrics and containing weak attempts at depth or humor: "You light my fire and make it Blase." Gifts from Agnes—a pair of silk boxers covered with hearts and, on a label sewn inside the waistband, one of her many "I ♥ U"s which could also be found inscribed in every book she gave him, like *How to Write a Novel*, *How to Publish Fiction in a Factual World*, and other volumes whose titles must have made him cringe. Empty vials of cocaine.

For a while I considered revenge. I gathered all the junk Blase had left behind, piled it in the living room, and debated setting it on fire. I penned blackmail notes and letters to his parents telling all. I might even phone Agnes, let her know what sort of person she was really involved with, as if this were something I knew. I even considered suing Blase for putting me at risk for AIDS, which he may or may not have done. I'd tested negative so far but no one was really sure about the incubation period. Blase would deny all, of course, but there was the material evidence of the note from James Hartley. I rifled through Blase's socks and pockets, checked under the mattress, ripped the linings out of his blazers, shook out every book we owned, tore his study apart, but no note. Apparently Blase had been farsighted enough to destroy it. But I could call James. Oh, yes I could. Then I could sue. James's testimony would be evidence enough. I'd take all of Blase's money and leave him alone and humiliated in the cold light of public scrutiny. But sue for what? *He betrayed me, Your Honor. He lied to me. He changed. He stopped loving me, Your Honor.* As far as I knew, being an asshole still wasn't a crime.

Finally I realized that even if there were some old statute that could be dusted off and pointed at him like a gun, revenge wasn't really what I wanted. What I wanted was to change the past, to make the world a world in which Blase hadn't become a poseur, returned to drugs, turned away from me, received such a note from James Hartley, left me for Agnes. And how could inflicting pain on Blase ever make the world a world like that?

Maybe it was Aristotle who said, "For this is lacking even to God: to make undone things that have once been done." Something like that.

"I was wondering were you okay?" Zara, the cleaning woman, person, whatever.

"What do you mean?"

"Every time I come and here you are in your nightgown still, sitting here on the floor, drinking wine," she said. "I don't think this is so good. I don't think the wine is so good."

Naturally, I fired her. And, also naturally, I avoided the confrontation by telling her I could no longer afford her services.

✻   ✻   ✻

After Blase had left, taken my whole life with him, I felt justified in letting go of everything. I stopped opening mail. Making lists. Paying bills. I didn't make or answer phone calls. I didn't even brush my hair. After Blase's supply ran out, I ordered a case of wine from a liquor store. We'd made it through the "for worse" part. We'd made it through the "for poorer" part. We'd never had to deal with the "in sickness" part. But somehow we hadn't been able to endure the "for richer" stage of our marriage. We'd said we'd do it. We'd promised. Until death.

Funny, just when you've comforted yourself with the thought that things are so bad they couldn't possibly get worse, things seem to get worse. And maybe you even wonder if it's all over—while it's really quite possible that things are getting better, only you can't recognize it because you're so accustomed to viewing everything through a glass, darkly, as the saying goes.

After days of sitting on the floor, drinking wine, staring at the front door, trying to force it to open and show me Blase outside, on his knees, penitent, sweet, the old Blase, I decided that the end had come, my end. Really, I thought about it this way, in hammy, histrionic clichés. We had a grand love and I wasn't going to allow that it had atrophied or, worse, that it had been illusory. Blase was my dearly beloved, the love of my life, my essence. His heart was my heart. His soul was my soul. I knew him as I knew myself. I was no one without him.

I turned on the bathwater. "Yes, it's the end," I said, and I squeezed a few tears out of my eyes. I put

Patsy Cline on the stereo and took a good look at the living room. "This will be the last time I see this place," I said, "this furniture." Skinny lamps, fat couches. Pillars. Two gold-leaf rococo mirrors. "Hideous," I said.

"The last time I hear this sad song," but Patsy came out with a jaunty little tune about smokin' cigarettes on a Saturday night instead of "Sweet Dreams." I flipped the tape.

On the side table, a scrapbook. I ran my finger along the edge of the cover, then opened it. Surely it contained glimpses of the past that would expand and deepen the mood I was trying to create. There I was, sitting with Blase at some restaurant. A fan was blowing on us and I was pleased to see that my hair looked rather wild, sexy even, while the wave at the side of Blase's head was standing up like a sail. "That was a great dress," I said, wondering what had happened to it.

I stroked the surface of the dining room table, the backs of the chairs. "I'll never dine at this table again," I said, but then I remembered I never *had* dined at the table. Blase and I always ate in the kitchen. As far as I knew the only ingestion that had taken place in this room had been of drugs and alcohol. "I will never dine at this table."

Little Blase on the beach with his doggy. "You were the best part of me," I said. Then I ground my thumb into his face. I looked at all the windup toys, picked up the chattering teeth, which I'm sure I would have addressed, such was my frame of mind, if they hadn't begun to bite in my hand. "Disgusting."

I was ready to wax metaphorical about the moribund living urn plant but saw that it had been removed from the windowsill. "Gone, just like our love." I winced.

I peered into the bedroom. I waited. No wistful, nostalgic thoughts came to me. Nothing much had ever happened here.

I opened the door to the guest room. "Good riddance!" I shouted.

The tub was full.

I took a new razor from the package of disposables in the medicine cabinet. I eased into the water.

"This toilet, this sink—these will be the last things I ever see," I said, lifting my feet out of the water and pressing them on either side of the faucet. "And these toenails."

"I'll never taste food or smell flowers." I soaped up my left leg. No excuse for being in the bathtub with a razor and having hairy legs. I nicked my knee, so I had to get out of the tub and search the drawers of the vanity until I found the styptic pencil.

Then I soaped my right leg.

"I'll never hear another song, or the phone's ring, or Blase's stupid laugh."

The phone rang. Then two more times. I strained to hear the message, but the answering machine didn't pick up. I grabbed a towel and ran into the kitchen. The machine was on. I slid the volume button to "MAX." You never knew when an emergency might come up.

The water had cooled so I began to drain it, then plugged it again and added more hot.

I stepped back into the tub.

The phone. Then Isabelle's voice: "Hey, sis. It's your older and wiser sister, Iz. If you don't call me *tonight*, I swear I'm beelining it to that sewer city you call home. This is not an idle threat." She paused. "You're really not there? Shit. Look, call me. I'm worried about you."

How sweet of Iz to care. She'd miss me for sure, but she'd get over it. That's one of the tragedies of life, I thought, that the horror of tragedy fades, simply by becoming old news. I suspected I could work out some kind of infinite regress about tragedies here, but then I saw the razor again, sitting patiently in the soap dish.

I stared at the razor, grabbed it and raised it in the air.

"Oh, happy dagger!" I actually said.

I brought the razor to my wrist, closed my eyes, and pushed down. I didn't feel anything. When I looked at my wrist, it was smooth; only a few tiny blond hairs on the razor blade. I closed my eyes again and pushed down harder this time. I felt the sting and brought my wrist before my eyes. Closer. And there it was, a cut. A short red line. "The beginning of the end," I said, and pulled my arm underwater. Then I tried to decide what I wanted my last words to be.

I'd once read a book of famous last words and now I remembered a few. The last words of an eighteenth-century socialite, demonstrating a new pistol: "Here's one you've never seen before." While peering over a parapet during some battle, an American Civil War general said, "They couldn't

243

hit an elephant at this dist—" And my favorite though whose they were I couldn't say: "Either that wallpaper goes, or I do." But what was the point of last words when there was no one around to record them?

"I am alone," I said, and I waited, but it didn't bring tears. "I am *all* alone." I didn't want to have to resort to "Nobody loves me" because I knew it wasn't true and thinking about the people who loved me—Claire, my sisters, David, my mother and father, even—would definitely spoil the mood. "I am *dying* alone." But was it true? When I raised my arm from the water to check my progress, the cut wasn't bleeding. It was just a rosy little line, a tiny irritation, like a kitten's scratch. I pressed it, but I couldn't get it to bleed again. "Even at the end, I am faced with disappointment."

I rubbed at my wrist until a small crimson drop began to form along the pink line. I lowered my arm into the water again.

The phone again?

"Della Kramer speaking. I was thinking that, man, you really should consider writing on some of the stuff Nagel's working on—*Mortal Questions*, you know? Like 'Sexual Perversion,' 'What Is It Like to Be a Bat?', 'Brain Bisection and the Unity of Consciousness,' or maybe 'Moral Luck.' "

She was still talking but I couldn't hear her. I was miles away. *Moral luck.* Now that was something I'd read once. That was something that had mattered to me, something I'd thought about, cared about, in a personal way.

What was it Nagel had said? It seemed to be something like this: A person can be a good person, lead a sterling moral life, simply because he's had great moral luck. He's never been profoundly tempted—by an open vault in an empty bank, or by having to choose between defending the lives of his near and dear and saving his own ass. That kind of thing.

Maybe that's what Blase had had. *Bad moral luck.* Blase.

Blase would come home and find me like this, in a tub of red liquid, cold and lifeless—"Toby, darling!"—and he would drop to his knees, sobbing, realizing how much he had loved me and that he couldn't go on without me. He'd open the medicine cabinet, fill his palm with pills, and swallow them. No. As far as Blase was concerned, drugs were for recreational use only. But he'd always loved Japanese films, so probably he'd hurry to the kitchen and grab the carving knife and thrust it into his stomach—no, Blase had always been a baby about pain, so probably not seppuku. Somehow, he'd get a gun. Yes, like Hemingway, he'd put the barrel of a loaded shotgun in his mouth—*but would he?*

I want you to remember this . . . so one day you can tell my biographer.

Then I saw him walking into the bathroom, spotting me in the blood-dimmed water, dashing to the phone—and calling the papers. There'd be a big to-do about the famous writer's crazy wife's suicide and everyone would feel sorry for Blase, who'd be giving out lots of interviews about the tragedy (wearing dark shades: "She lost her mind," "I did all I could for her," "My heart is broken," *snap*) and who'd be selling even more books and understandably seeking comfort from his close friend, starlet Agnes Airhead, and everyone would be so happy for him when he finally overcame his grief and married the kind, sympathetic woman playing the June Allyson role.

"No *way*." I rose from the tub. "No fucking *way*."

The phone again. A woman's voice on the answering machine.

A voice I didn't recognize. I ran for it.

"Hello I'm here," I blurted.

"Toby Regenhere?"

"Yes."

"This is Marion Hadley from Bell Press."

"Bell Press?"

"Yes. You sent us some material a few months ago," the woman said.

"I did?" My cartoons. Someone was calling me about my cartoons. "Oh, yes."

"I'm sure you received our correspondence." The mail. Since Blase left I hadn't checked the mail. "When I phoned a couple of weeks ago your husband said you'd be able to make it in today."

"What time?"

"I was expecting you at noon," the woman said. She paused. "But I could see you in an hour, if you're free."

"I'm free," I said.

"You understand: we can't use what you sent us, but we're interested in discussing another project with you."

I replaced the receiver.

I was standing naked in a puddle of water.

"Yes!" I said, and high-fived myself. I did a little dance around the living room.

As I was dressing, occasionally rising and saying, "Yes!" at myself in the wall mirror, the phone rang again.

"How you doing?"

"Blase?"

"Is everything okay?"

"Fine," I said.

"That's good," he said, but he sounded disappointed. He was calling from a phone booth. I could hear the street sounds: trucks, cars, a siren. "Want to have dinner tonight?" I heard a snap, even with all the midday midtown noise.

"With you?"

"Yeah." Snap.

Honestly, there was a part of me that wanted to say yes, part of me that still wanted to go back to that dingy little Indian restaurant downtown and fall in love with him all over again.

I glanced across the dining room. The bathroom door was open. There was the tub, filled with water. Cold water by now.

"I don't think so," I said.

"*No?*"

I, or part of me, wanted to say, "Yes! I meant *yes.*" Part of me wanted to be holding his hand, strolling by the river, dreaming dreams. Part of me wanted to forget his nightclubbing, the drugs, the note from James Hartley, Agnes.

But then I realized it wasn't *part* of me that had these feelings, they belonged to *me* as a unity, as a whole thing; I simply didn't have them wholeheartedly.

"Are you saying *no*?"

"Yes," I said. "I'm saying no."

I was shaking when I got off the phone.

I'd said no. Maybe it was a mistake. Didn't I love him? Not the new Blase, the puffed-up, shallow, slick, adulterous Blase, but the *real* Blase who'd once loved me.

For a while I thought about the old Blase as if, despite all the changes, despite all the new experiences, there were a tiny Blase, the true one, solid, immutable, behind the scenes, making all the choices, pulling all the strings. Maybe the new Blase was the same as the old Blase, it's just that in these new circumstances, he wasn't a very good puppeteer. He'd had bad moral luck.

Then it occurred to me that the old Blase couldn't be the new Blase because the old Blase would never have treated me badly. Maybe a person is not a stable thing, but changes with each new experience, with each day, each moment; it's just that we only note it, call it "a profound change," when it affects us profoundly. To love someone for the rest of your life isn't just to love the person with whom you exchange I do's, but to love the persons he will be. Maybe this was true. Maybe this was one reason why marriages so often fail: it isn't that the husband and wife fall out of love, but that they just don't love the new husband or wife the old one has become.

Or perhaps while the new Blase wasn't the old Blase, he could be the old Blase again if he so chose. Or maybe the new Blase wasn't the old Blase and there was no getting back from here to there. Maybe, maybe, maybe.

I thought myself round and round this question of who Blase really was until I realized I didn't know who Blase was or who he had been. I didn't know whether we'd ever really shared dreams, whether he'd even liked the country, whether he'd ever really wanted a family. I didn't know whether we really looked alike, whether this was one reason he'd wanted to marry me. I really didn't know whether he'd been trying to drive me crazy. Whether he'd secretly, really, wanted us to be Scott and Zelda. Whether he was gay or bisexual or in love with Agnes.

But did it matter whether Blase had been like this all along or whether he'd changed? Did it matter whether, in these circumstances, Blase would inevitably become who he now appeared to be? I didn't even *like* who he now appeared to be, I knew *that*, and that's what mattered.

I had spent so long trying to answer Wittgenstein's challenge—*how do you know?*—evoking theories of meaning and reference, grappling with truth and Tarski's schema, and really, finally, all that I could say was, I do not know how I know, I only know. And *whereof one cannot speak, thereof one must be silent.*

I had once thought knowledge was a simple thing, a matter of feeling certain, a matter of having some justification, some evidence, a few good reasons. But like a many-arrowed sign at a crossroads, evidence can point this way and that way and that. We can misread it, misuse it in our reasoning. I'd leave it to the philosophers, mathematicians, and scientists to work out which were the dead ends and which were routes leading to the profound truths. For now, I'd accept that I had my beliefs, my memories, and that from these I could construct a story that seemed coherent, that made sense to me, though whether the story was *true* I'd probably never know, and maybe that was itself a piece of knowledge, and maybe it was good enough for now.

Then I thought of my mother, whom I'd been so angry at for so long—not as she was now, tired and sad and lonely, but as she had been when I was growing up and she was living on gin and resentment, blaming us for her unhappy childhood and her unhappy marriage. I dialed her number.

"*Where* have you been?"

"I've just been settling in," I said. "Readjusting to life without Blase."

"Life without Blase?"

I paused. "He left."

"Honey, I'm so sorry," she said.

I'd thought she was going to say she'd always known he was a worm. I'd thought she was going to point out that it was just like an Episcopalian to dump his wife. I'd thought she was going to add something about my being better off without him, but she said, "Are you all right?"

"Fine," I said. "Really."

"Is there anything I can do?"

"No. Thanks. I'm okay."

"You sure?" Mom asked.

"Positive."

"Well, just let me know."

"Mom? I'm really sorry about missing your birthday."

"Don't be ridiculous," she said. She paused. "You know, Toby, I always knew Blase was a louse."

After I'd dug my portfolio from the back of the hall closet, locked the door, and rung for the elevator, it suddenly struck me that maybe in saying no to Blase I'd thrown something away, something I'd never have a chance at again. I saw us holding hands across a restaurant table, gazing into each other's eyes. By the river, just discovering each other, each one asking, "Could it be *you*?" Then I was in the Philosophy Graduate Fellows office and the deejay was saying, "I have a special message from Blase to Toby: 'This song is dedicated to you, sweetheart, and so am I,' " and then "When a Man Loves a Woman" beginning to play. Opening a card from Blase, glitter falling to the floor. Blase on one knee, on the sidewalk, offering me a flower he'd just swiped from someone's window box, saying, "My love is like a purple, purple pansy." Strolling around Beekman Place hand in hand; slurping oysters at Grand Central; trying not to laugh at some of the New Art in Greenwich Village galleries.

Blase toasting me: "Had I the Heavens' embroidered clothes . . . I would spread the cloths under your feet." Then, talking together of our future, our home in the country, taking turns adding each sparkling detail—"A barn," Blase said, "with two horses"; "Three," I said, "one for our kids. And a vegetable garden with tomatoes and stringbeans and lettuce"; "Five kinds of lettuce," Blase said—building a dream together.

I heard the phone ringing from my apartment.

Maybe it was Blase.

Ring.

Maybe he wanted to give it another try.

I put my key back in the lock.

Behind me, the elevator door slid open.

The phone was ringing.

I turned, then stepped into the elevator.

The phone was still ringing.

Maybe we *could* start over, build something different, something real, solid, immutable.

I remembered part of a sonnet:

And ruined love, when it is built anew,
Grows fairer than at first, more strong, far greater.

For a long moment, the doors remained open, the phone ringing from far away.

Maybe we could begin again and maybe it would be even better this time.

No, *that* was the illusion—not that that time had been real, but that it was something we could possibly have again.

I pushed "one" and the doors slid quietly into place.